Paper Wings

Linda Sargent was born and brought
up in Kent and now lives and works
in Oxfordshire.

Paper Wings

by Linda Sargent

OMNES

Set in Sorts Mill Goudy
Cover design by Hannah Firmin

In memory of Reg Sells

Ghost Walker

It was a time when you could get lost in the wood, or live in it for years without being much noticed; people did, then. Looking at it from a high point not far away, where in the distance you might glimpse the thin line of sea glimmering between land and sky, from here the trees massed thick and solid, as if a patched blanket of shifting, changing greens had been cast over the ground at the farm's edge, reaching almost to the sea itself.

And this was the time of wound licking. The bombings, the murders, the clashing of armies, had ended, yet the rawness and the damage they had brought were still there, not far from the surface of things. Staying out of sight and away from the judgement of others was one way of trying to heal. All that was needed was somewhere safe to hide. The wood, it seemed then, was such a place.

The farm

When she heard the shot Ruby ran to the door and would have
run on and out down to the bottom of the garden, if her mum
hadn't stopped her. At that moment she hated them both, Dad
for what he'd done and Mum for not letting her go and take one
last look at Blackness.

"Not now," her mum said, holding her by the shoulders, "best
to remember her as she was, eh?"

Ruby struggled free and ran off upstairs, not to her bedroom,
but to the attic, burying her face into the blanket where
Blackness used to sleep, filling her memory with the smell of
her, scraping the dark hairs into a small ball to make a keepsake
for her locket, like they did in the stories. She sobbed and
sobbed until the effort of it exhausted her and she fell asleep,
not even hearing her mum come up and cover her properly with
one of the blankets from her bed.

The next day, Saturday, her dad was busy in the shed all morning, sawing and hammering and just before dinner time he
called her to come and have a look.

Ruby traced her fingers round the shape in the lid and looked
up at her dad who was busy cleaning his chisel. "S'like she's
asleep," she said, still running her fingers round the edges, "the
way she always sleeps."

"Slept." Her dad's voice was soft in the shed's dusty light.

"Slept," repeated Ruby.

"Shall I carve her name now, then?"

"Yes," she said and watched as he chipped and cut the B and
the other eight letters as carefully as if the wood might be alive.

While he dug the hole underneath the apple tree, Ruby said a

9

prayer, the Lord's Prayer, the one they did every morning at school; it was the only one she knew all the way through off by heart. Then she played a tune on her xylophone, The Bluebells of Scotland, which like the prayer, she could do from memory.

"Blackness would like that, I reckon," her dad said, after they'd stood silent for a moment or two, him holding his cap squashed together, bare headed out of respect.

"Yes," Ruby said, kneeling down to place the bunch of raggedy dog roses on the newly dug hump, a stray petal loosening in the breeze and drifting off into the hedge like a straggle of confetti, or like tiny angel wings Ruby thought and it cheered her.

"D'you think she'll get wings?" she asked her mum later, while they were pegging out the washing together.

"Who?"

"Blackness, in heaven, you know if she turns into an angel?"

"Well, maybe," her mum said, a mouth full of pegs. "You never know what might happen I suppose. Anything's possible." It was one of Mum's favourite sayings. Ruby considered the idea.

"She could fly then," she whispered, but this time to herself.

"Angels, eh?" she overheard her dad say as she was practising her three-ball near the back door.

"Well," her mum answered, "wished I'd still thought I might see the odd angel or two when I was nine." This was followed by a hefty sigh and Ruby guessed that her mum was most likely thinking of her own dad, who'd been killed, or 'lost' it said on the piece of paper she'd seen. Lost? In that first war, the long ago war, not the one that was still fresh in all the grown-ups' heads because it had, after all, only ended fourteen years ago, the year Blackness was born.

Ruby never tired of hearing the story of Blackness' birth, of how her mother Tibby, when she was just about to have her litter, had crept under the fallen half-rotted tree trunk in the cherry orchard, just over the stile at the bottom of the garden; near enough to safety but on the edge of the wild too. That's what

Ruby's dad said, how animals, even cats, still had a bit of wild in them and needed to remember it sometimes. Tibby had only birthed two kittens that time and one of them, a tom, had died soon afterwards. Dad had told her it was because Tibby was getting nearly too old to have kittens and, in fact, a year later she too had died, leaving only Blackness who was five the year Ruby herself was born. They even shared the same birthday. Strange. June 21st. And soon it would be her birthday, but not Blackness'.

She left her balls by the water butt and ran down again to where the grave was. Ruby dropped to her knees and felt the warm tears on her face. It wasn't fair, they'd always been together for their birthdays and now it would be her on her own. Having Blackness was almost as good as having a sister. Being an only child could often be a lonely business.

"Ruby?"

She wiped her face on the sleeve of her cardigan, hating it when he saw her cry.

"Sorry about Blackness, my mum's just told me."

How come he didn't hear the shot? Was what she was thinking, but didn't say. Peter sometimes did things like that, pretended, hid bad happenings by the words he used, like he was protecting her. Ruby thought it could be because he was older, eleven at the end of September, when she was not quite ten yet. If Blackness had been her imagined sister, Peter might be her brother. She'd known him all her life too, he lived next door; they'd started school at the same time, learnt to ride bikes at the same time, scrumped apples from the farm next door, started digging to Australia. Sharing it all, the two of them. Sharing being the only child in their families too, which made it all the more special. His dad did an important job on the farm, looking after the pigs and sheep, her dad was in charge of the hops; the way it had always been.

"Dad had to do it," Ruby said, still kneeling.

"I know."

"It was rat poison, most likely."

"Yes." Peter knelt and straightened the tiny makeshift cross Ruby had stuck in the earth.

"She was frothing at the mouth, green foamy stuff, really sick. I hate rats."

"So do I." He stood up, brushing dirt from his hands.

"Poor Blackness." Ruby couldn't help it then, not just tears but heaving sobs pushed out of her making it hard to breathe. Peter pulled a large, surprisingly white, handkerchief from his pocket, handed it to her and walked across to the swing, where he sat, swinging gently to and fro, staring absently up through the branches of the apple tree at the patched blue sky, whistling softly between his teeth, waiting for Ruby to buck up.

In the wood

It had been a long, long while since he'd been back here. The last time it had been open to the sky, the trees and the undergrowth still mashed and broken. Now, in that way that nature has, the wildness was taking over again. Beech saplings were beginning to grow around the edge of the clearing, that could now hardly be called such. Brambles had snatched the opportunity to fill up some of the gaps and, judging by the look of them, would be smothered in blackberries come September. He pulled some of them back though, wondering if there was material left that could be salvaged and of use to him. A stupid thought, perhaps, after sixteen years, but you never knew. After all, this good strong steel would last a lifetime and more. It was becoming increasingly difficult too, stealing and spiriting away those useful carelessly left-out items from barns and sheds. It was how he'd come by the gun and the ammunition. Twice, though, recently, he had nearly been seen and rooted instinct told him that he must never be seen because then they would surely come after him.

At that moment he heard the whistle and for a second believed that he was being watched. There! He glanced up, shielding his eyes from the sudden brightness that spilled through the opening; then he laughed. He called her in his own language, Little One; it was a name full of lonely memories. She must have followed him and he hadn't even noticed. A good trick, he thought, for a creature that was more at home in open clearer spaces than in the secret hidden places of the wood – his wood, was how he described it to himself. She would have had to track him by glimpse and guess work. He whistled back to her and she hovered for a brief span before moving off and then down, arrow quick, having spotted prey now.

He wished her luck, silently, thinking of the cold meat he'd stashed away waiting for him when he returned. Now to business. He climbed up slow and gentle on to what was left of the plane's wings.

The farm

"Can you fasten them on for me?" Ruby had checked that the glue was really dry this time and handed the wings to Peter. She'd made some holes and threaded elastic through so they could be looped round her shoulders.

"How's that feel?" He was frowning, making sure they looked level.

"Bit tight really." Ruby sighed and slipped them off. "And shouldn't I be able to flap them?" She squinted up at Peter, who had climbed up on to the stile and was practising standing on one leg.

"Suppose." He dropped down and took them from her.

"D'you think it's because they're not real?"

"Well, maybe – "

Ruby sighed again. It was no good, when it came to it these angel wings were never going to work, flying was for birds, angels and fairies – if you believed in fairies. These wings, when Ruby first saw them on the back of a magazine advertising – now what had it been, cooking fat? – had looked so convincing, as if the broad gold feathers might have slipped from the back of a passing angel.

Now, though; well they seemed stiff and lifeless, paper on cardboard, no more. With about as much chance of flying as one of Peter's paper aeroplanes, less probably.

Next week was her birthday and she knew what she was going to wish for, same as she wished every year, but this time it would come true. She was certain.

"Dad says some more stuff has gone missing from the cold store, well, the tractor shed." Peter sat on the stile now and was gently lifting the drawn feathers with his penknife, but they still looked like paper.

"Oh?" Ruby squinted up at the piled clouds, pushing higher into the blue, they really did seem like mountains. How amazing it would be if they were real, just down there, past the Ten Acre hop garden, follow the line of trees up the hill to the edge of Bower Wood, over a hundred acres her dad said. That was big; Ruby wondered why it wasn't called a forest. Imagine if stretching towards heaven, those clouds were actual mountains. She sighed.

"You still missing Blackness?" Peter carried on slipping the knife between the paper feathers, he was never one to give up once he'd decided.

Ruby nodded, she still couldn't talk about Blackness without the tears coming. Funny, though, Peter asking like that. Unusual for him, she squinted at him now.

"Was it the Ghost Man?"

"Huh?"

"Taking things? From the cold store?"

"Ghosts don't need to steal." He cleaned his knife on his trousers and pushed it into his pocket.

"Who, then?" He was in a funny mood, normally he'd have agreed. The Ghost Man was the name they always used, although Ruby's dad said, whenever things went missing, that it was mostly likely the travellers, the gypsies who came for casual work and sometimes returned when no one was looking to help themselves to fruit and other bits and pieces, having sussed where things were kept and who was likely to be around when and who not.

Yet, it was the Ghost Man who kept them from going too far into the woods, him and all the wells that waited, unused for years, hidden in the undergrowth, there to tilt you down into a dark and watery death.

Peter shrugged. "Fancy a bike ride?"

Ruby picked up the wings and followed him along the path.

The Leas

No real direction in mind, in the end they decided to cycle up across the gooseberry field along the track that ended at the shop on the Leas. Peter had some money, enough to buy them both a cornet and a gobstopper each. They sat outside on the low wall eating their ice creams, watching a bunch of other kids they knew playing on the swings in the playing field, not wanting to join in especially. From inside they could hear Mr. Harris, the shopkeeper, talking to another customer.

"Yes, that Bower Wood," he was saying. Peter nudged Ruby and they carried on licking at their cornets in silence.

"Gyppos, Stan reckons." It was old Mrs. Pierce from Mulberry Cottage. Stan was her son who sometimes helped out on the farm.

"Could be a blooming army living in there and we'd never know, eh?" Mr. Harris laughed.

"Can't leave anything lying about these days," Mrs. Pierce grumbled on.

"What's been taken this time, then?"

"Cartridges."

Mr. Harris whistled through his teeth, it was something he was known for. "Blimey."

"Someone forgot to lock the cupboard in the cold store, Stan says."

"Someone's going to be in trouble then, eh, Mrs. P?"

"Could be murdered in our beds."

"Us or them rabbits, eh?" Peter and Ruby could hear Mr. Harris shaking up the sweet jars, and then the creak of the scales, Mrs. Pierce must be buying her usual quarter of mint humbugs.

"Ah, well, better be getting on. Stan'll be home for tea soon."

Peter joggled his head to and fro, mouthing the words again and Ruby giggled. He was a good mimic.

"You never said it was cartridges," she said as they wheeled their bikes back along the track.

He shrugged. "Didn't know. What's it matter anyway?"

"They're not going to shoot us?"

"Who?"

"The gypsies?" She thought about Oby, who was in her class, how he'd once picked up the sixpence she'd dropped and given it to her.

"Don't be daft." Peter swung back on his bike. "Come on. Race you to the Big Fir!"

"Lookout branch?" Ruby knew that would slow him down. Winning the bike race was one thing, climbing the Big Fir something he generally left to her and in her mind's eye she was already there, swinging among the branches, climbing higher and higher.

Bumping back across Roman Fields Ruby pedalled hard while way, way above somewhere a sky lark sang as it flew up into the swiped-clean blue air.

In the wood

Although the gypsies came and went in the woods, they mostly kept to the area next to the hop gardens. Habit, he supposed, since it was there they camped during the picking season and sometimes earlier in the year, during the spring when the young bines needed training up the newly strung poles. As far as he knew they didn't know he was there, or at least if they did, he wasn't someone they considered to be significant in their lives. He guessed they must often take the blame for some of his stealing, but nothing ever seemed to come of it so, after a while, he stopped worrying. The wood was big enough for those who chose to stay or pass through to remain invisible if they wished.

Several times recently, though, he had felt – imagined, perhaps? – that he had been watched when usually it was he who was the watcher. Today had been one of those moments, but he couldn't really explain why; there'd been no sign of anyone, no sound of twigs breaking underfoot, no rustling undergrowth, no signals from animals or birds that a stranger, or strangers were near, no shadows among the trees apart from those that belonged there. And yet: it was as if someone – something – might be on the brink of whispering in his ear. Once he caught the end of a sentence, he thought he heard his name and he half turned in the dusk-shadowed copse where he'd come to fetch water from one of the hidden wells. His name? And something else too, words he hardly recognised, it having been so long since he'd heard them spoken aloud and to him. These days even his dreams were a strange mixture of his present older and past younger self.

"Gabriel, Gabriel." There it was again, sifting through the still evening light, his name like a finger being lifted and pointed. Accusing. It was, he now understood, a voice he recognised, one he hadn't heard for fifteen years. He turned.

"My God!" he said. "It is you."

The sea

Ruby's chosen birthday treat was a trip to Seashell Flats, although it had to be the day before because her actual birthday fell on a Monday that year. School, which meant everyone would sing at her and then, later, in the playground, she'd have the bumps. She might get to decide the game too, and it would be rounders, it was always rounders when Ruby had the chance.

Today, though, everything was for her and she and Peter could do whatever they wanted; eat ice cream before sandwiches, play French Cricket, make her dad join in, splash about by the break-water, wander as far as they liked – almost – when the tide went out and collect cockles to keep or give away to the serious hunt-ers. It didn't matter, it was a magic time and Ruby had woken up that morning, checking her shoulder blades as usual, hoping, just hoping that the wings her mum reckoned could be there somewhere, might be starting to show.

Nothing, as usual, so she'd have to make do, as always, with jumping off the sea wall, flapping her arms as fast as she could and feeling the sudden breathy lift of the wind as she went down, so that for a small, tantalizing moment, she was almost flying.

"You be careful!" Her mum's voice mixed in with the seagull cries and the slow dragging wash of the waves.
    "Coming?" Ruby nudged Peter, who was standing next to her. He never jumped, well, hardly ever, just like he never climbed trees unless the branches were really solid and not too far from the ground.
    "All right." That was a surprise.
    "One! Two! Three! Go!"

Later, while they were sitting on the breakwater, feeling the roll-ing push of the water up to their knees, Peter pulled an envelope from his pocket.
    "Forgot to give it to you this morning. Sorry."
    "S'all right." Ruby opened it.
    "Careful."
    "Oh." She'd been expecting a card, something his mum would have most likely bought for him to give to her. But it wasn't a card, it was a feather. White, long and beautiful,

smooth as silk to touch.

"It's a swan's feather," he said.

"It's lovely," Ruby said, stroking it and knowing it was most likely one of his treasures. Peter was always picking up odd bits and pieces, skeleton leaves, frail as spider's web, flints, fossils they called Shepherd's Crowns, starfish thousands of years dead, imprinted forever on the round stones sometimes turned up by the plough. It was rare for him to give one of these precious objects to someone else.

"I found it up on the Mound." He had picked up a pebble and now skimmed it across the water.

"Thanks." Ruby stared at it, trying to imagine having a load of these fixed together on the thin bony shape of complete wings.

"Couldn't see anymore, though, but I didn't have time to check the caves."

Ruby nodded, the caves were out of bounds, but that didn't stop them going there when they felt daring enough to break the rules. Part of an old chalk diggings, most of them didn't go back very far, but there was one that did, stretching back and down into darkness where they sometimes came across dead animals and birds.

"Most likely just this one, though." He'd picked up another stone and was busy aiming it to spin across the foamy lick of the waves. Just then Ruby's mum started calling them for tea and cake and Ruby could see her dad coming down the wooden steps carrying the buckets ready for the cockle hunt later.

That night in the kitchen, Ruby was washing some of the shells she and Peter had collected, while her mum sorted out the towels for the copper wash the next day. Searching in her pocket for more shells, Ruby found the feather again and took it out to show her mum.

"Peter gave it to me." She smoothed it from where it had gone ragged, scrunched in with the shells and her handkerchief.

"Peter gave you what?" Her dad had come in with a bowl of

new potatoes, freshly dug, the smell was sharp and summery.

"This," said Ruby, handing him the feather.

Even when she told Peter the next day (her actual birthday) as they walked up through Roman Fields to catch the school bus from the Leas, even then she still couldn't work it out.

"What do you mean, he was cross?" Peter was walking backwards ahead of her.

"He asked me why you'd given it to me."

"Perhaps he was worried about germs, or something?"

"Perhaps," she said, but she knew that wasn't the reason, that whatever it was that made her dad look at her with such unfamiliar eyes, as if she was a stranger who'd no business to be in their kitchen, or as if she done something so bad there were no words for it. Whatever it was, it wasn't about germs, nothing so ordinary.

And after she'd gone to bed her mum had come in very quietly to check if she was asleep and although Ruby had wanted to ask her why Dad had been so angry and why he'd stormed off out to the pub and still wasn't back, she couldn't find the right words.

The saddest thing of all was the way her dad had thrown the feather into the fire before she'd had a chance to grab it back from him and it had been that which had made her cry.

The Mound

He didn't often come up here, it was too exposed, he could easily be seen if anyone happened to be passing, but it was such a soft warm evening, so inviting, he couldn't resist. From here he could catch a rare sight of the sea, a thin lick of silver on the horizon that made him, more than anything, think of home. Yet, in truth, his home was far from the sea. Strange, that. And the caves below; years before he'd considered them as possible shelter, but soon decided that the wood offered better protection. He knew that children often played here and it was too risky.

Tonight, though, tonight was different and ever since he'd heard that voice he felt compelled to come out of the wood for a while, into the clearer un-haunted air.

"Gabriel." The sound of his voice speaking his own name floated back at him like a half remembered object from childhood.

He looked down at the farm, a picture-book spread of fields, orchard, buildings, hop gardens. How real it all was, how close, but for him, how far too. There were nights, in winter mostly, when he would wander around just for the sensation of being there and of reminding himself that he was alive, he had survived all that horror, he could still see, walk, breathe, touch, hear and be real. Sometimes, when he thought back to that past it was as if it had happened to another, it might have been a story he'd heard and marvelled at, things he had been told, a kind of fairy tale. It was so fantastic.

Then he remembered what he had done and why he could never go home.

The school

Ruby was balancing on the top bar of the climbing frame. From here she could see over the wall into the castle grounds, it all looked so tidy and proper, like the gardens in the Sleeping Beauty story, before the wicked fairy's spell; lawns and lawns, edged with rose beds, small ponds and big ponds, fountains that glittered like careless treasure and at the head of it all, the house with too many windows to count, settled there and in charge of everything and everyone. Officially, Ruby had only ever been in there for village fetes; unofficially, she and Peter would occasionally creep in through a loose bit of fence down near the village hall and set up temporary camp near the old pig sties.

But that was only when they were feeling bored enough to be reckless. The penalty for trespassing was – well, she wasn't exactly sure, but she knew it would involve the police, even prison. Maybe.

"You coming down, or what?" Peter was squinting up at her. Standing next to him was Sally holding the rounders' bat, making pretend swipes. They were waiting to start the game.

Later, when they were putting things away in the store room, which everyone still called the Shelter and was also where Cook kept all the vegetables for dinners, Ruby talked to Peter about the feather again.

"I still don't get it." He pulled a couple of potatoes from a sack and started juggling with them. Then took another, managing several goes without dropping one.

"He was cross," she shrugged, mostly she'd got over it now, but was still a bit confused. She half hoped Peter might know the reason.

"Beats me," he shook his head and dropped the potatoes back into their sack. "I'll try and get you another one." He frowned into the dark passage as if there might be a swan's wing hidden amongst the vegetables. "Come on." He headed for the doorway. But Ruby stood for a moment and looked back, shivering in the cool air, catching the earthy, familiar smell of the place thinking fleetingly, about all the people who would have sheltered here during the War, listening to the boom, boom of the bombs falling outside wondering if the next one might fall on them.

"Wait for me!" She skipped after him, back out into the warm afternoon light. One more lesson and it would be time to go home.

The caves

"Did you bring the torch?" Peter was already ahead of her, scrambling over the crumbling chunks of chalk and into the cave.

Ruby waved it at him and stuck her tongue out at his back. He could be bossy at times.

"Well, switch it on then!"

It was Saturday and they'd been hanging round the cherry orchard supposedly helping, but after a while eating too many for it not to be noticed and then being shooed off and told to Go off and play now!

And it had been Peter's idea to come up here and search for more swan's feathers. He was sure there'd be more and that most likely, if they looked in the caves they'd find them. Ruby waved the torch, sweeping its light up and down, and watching the patterns on the ragged walls.

"Point it down here, stupid!"

She pointed and waggled her tongue again, Peter didn't normally get so cross with her. Ruby sighed, though, and did as she was told.

"Over there – look!" She'd caught up with him and they'd gone so far in they were having to crouch now as the roof was low at this point. Ruby swung the torch up into his face and saw that he was sweating, yet it was so cold. Then she realised. He was scared.

"You all right?" It was a new thing, Peter being afraid.

"What?" He was kneeling now, tugging at something half buried by chalk rubble.

"You seem a bit – "

"Shine the bloody torch here!" He jabbed his fingers to show where.

Ruby knelt next to him and saw what he saw. "Ugh, it's dead. What is it?" Now she was afraid.

"Wings." His voice was all raspy from fear and chalk dust. "Swan's wings." And he smiled, rocking back on his heels, grinning at the strange luck of it.

Back outside, leaning against the grassy bank of the hill, Peter examined their find.

"How did it get there?" Ruby thought it looked less nasty now they could have a proper look at it out here in the thick afternoon sunlight; the caves seemed a long way away.

"Fox, most probably," Peter was still smoothing the feathers, amazed at how big the wings were, how complete and yet not, because the main thing that was missing was the swan itself.

"Blimey!"

"Must've been injured or something, though, I mean for a fox to get it. Big birds, swans, could break your arm, one of these."

Ruby stared trying to picture that scene, it was hard to imagine and yet they looked so frail and strong all at once. She wondered where the rest of the swan was, surely there'd be a head and legs – wouldn't there? It seemed funny that they'd found only the wings when wings were the very thing she wished for. All the time.

When Peter held the wings against her shoulder blades she wished there was a mirror so she could see properly, instead she jiggled, trying to peer at herself.

"Stand still!" Peter still sounded cross, she couldn't work it out, he was usually so steady.

"Sorry, I just wanted – "

"Oh, it's no good, I'll have to think of another way." He flumped down on the grass, pulling a strand and chewing on it, staring away towards the Bower woods.

Ruby wondered if she might go home if he was just going to be such a misery guts all of a sudden, but instead she sat down too.

"We'll have to hide them as well." He didn't look at her, but carried on scanning the distant mass of trees. "From your dad, I mean."

Ruby thought about this for a minute. Funny, the way her dad had been over the feather. She still couldn't work it out.

"S'pose so," she said.

Suddenly, Peter sat forward, frowning hard.

"What?" Ruby shaded her eyes.

"Thought so!" He stood up and was nodding to himself,

huffing in a satisfied way. He turned and glanced down at Ruby. "Smoke," he said, pointing, "see?"

And there, on the lip of the horizon where the wood seemed to roll towards the edge of the world, was a thin line of grey, like the wavering of a ghost's finger, disappearing up into the blue.

In the wood

He saw them before they realised he was even there, so he followed to see what they were doing. Soon he was close enough to hear what they were saying.

"We should have left them behind."

"The fox might have come back."

"Don't be daft, Ruby, he'd have taken them in the first place if he'd wanted to. We could have hidden them near the entrance. No one ever goes there in any case."

"I like wearing them, anyhow. I might have a go with them later." She squinted up at the trees. "If there's a tree I can climb."

Peter stopped right in front of her. "Listen."

She listened. It was still and quiet, except for the distant tap, tapping of a woodpecker away to their right and the thin papery whisper of leaves high up, shuffling gently in the lightest of breezes.

Behind them, their follower stopped too, crouching now, in case one of them turned round and saw him.

"What happens if we can't find our way out?" Ruby whispered.

"Shush!"

She tugged at her wings, loosening the string a little. Peter had tied it really tightly round her chest, to keep the wings in place. From a distance, if you didn't know better, she could almost be mistaken for an angel.

"I still don't know how you think we're going to find where the smoke was coming from." She was tired of this game, wanting to get to the important thing she had on her mind, which was trying out these real wings. The big pine back on the farm was really the best place, the grassy bank was thick and springy, always making a soft landing. And it was such an easy climb, she could almost do it with her eyes closed.

"The sun," Peter whispered back. "It's just a question of making sure it's in the right position."

Ruby giggled.

"What you laughing at?" Peter sounded puzzled and more like the old Peter, not the ratty one who'd come out of the caves.

"Don't know," she laughed, and it was true, she didn't. It was more like a feeling of relief suddenly, to find that he was himself again.

"Come on," he said, sighing as if he'd come out of a dream. "We'd better go, expect it's nearly tea time."

"You don't want to find the Ghost Man, then?"

"I've told you he's not – never mind."

"It might not have been him, that fire. Might have been the gypsies, Oby and all, you know."

"They don't normally go that far into the woods. Least, that's what I thought."

Just then they heard the crack of twigs behind them, Ruby grabbed Peter's sleeve and held on wanting to see, yet not wanting to see, who it was coming out of the shadows towards them.

"The man you look for is half an hour in that direction," Oby told them, pointing off to the right, "you were travelling the wrong way." He smiled, nodding hello to them. "Would you like to come down to the camp for some tea?"

The camp

Ruby felt a bit silly, sitting on the steps to Oby's caravan, with her wings still attached, while Mrs. Lee brewed the tea in a big old black can over the fire. This was the first time Oby had ever invited them, or anyone from school, to his camp and it felt special; she and Peter tried not to stare too much, but everything was all so strange, different and shining with dark earthy colours, that it was hard not to gape.

On the way there Oby had told them that it was best not to mention the Man; like Ruby, the gypsies called him Ghost Walker and for this reason steered clear of the places he was known to frequent. Ruby nudged Peter, who shrugged as if it didn't matter.

From where she sat Ruby could see the edge of the hop garden down the slope beyond the pond and a little further along to the left, the hut where her dad would have his lunch when he worked up at this end of the farm. She thought how strange it was that Oby's family and the others, had been here, watching, yet never being watched, like the Indians in the films, watching the wagon train. It made her shiver. Peter was jogging her arm and she realised Oby was asking her a question.

"Do you want sugar?"

"Mm?"

"In your tea?"

Afterwards, when they had eaten some of the boiled fruitcake, made by Oby's gran, who he said had gone to visit her other daughter down by the river on the edge of the village, he asked them if they'd like to look round.

"Won't they mind?" Peter said.

Oby frowned. "Mind?"

"The – your relations." He wasn't sure if this was right, but what else was he supposed to call them, these strange weather-browned people who seemed to find him and Ruby funny, or something, because he noticed how some of the smaller children ran behind them at a distance, mocking them by trying to copy the way they walked and the things they said.

"I think we should go soon," he whispered to Ruby, but she hadn't heard, because Oby was saying something to her that was making her clap her hand over her mouth in that way she had when she got excited about a new game. She and Oby started to run down towards the brook. "Come on!" Ruby called over her shoulder. "Oby's going to show us Nancy!"

Nancy lifted her head when Oby spoke her name. She was penned in by some jumbled together arrangement of old sheep hurdles and at one end was a roughly made lean-to for her shelter.

Ruby climbed up on the gate, next to Oby, "She's beautiful." Her voice now dropped to a rustling whisper. "Peter?"

He stayed where he was, shoving his hands into his pockets and poking at a pile of ancient leaf mulch with the toe end of his boot.

"Peter, don't you think she's just, just – "

Oby was grinning, proud and happy.

"Just what?" Peter said, looking up at last and squinting down through the bars at Nancy.

"Like something from a fairy tale." Ruby couldn't tear her eyes away.

"She's just a goat, you mean!" And straight away he was cross with himself because it was true, Nancy glowed white and mysterious, as if she might have been left there by a bunch of the little people.

"Why's she called Nancy?" He said, getting up next to them both, catching a sudden drift of the rich sharp smell of her.

"After my gran," Oby said.

"Blimey, she pongs though," Ruby said and they all laughed and it was better after that. Peter was no longer in such a hurry to leave and the three of them wandered along by the brook, dabbling sticks and watching for damsel flies, wondering if next time they could bring a fishing rod and try for some of the tiddlers that darted quick and black in the tree green water.

The Leas

It was the last day of term and the two of them were wandering hot and slow past the gooseberry field, stopping now and then to rummage for forgotten fruit, but mostly the bushes had been stripped and any left were soggy and split, like eating squishy lumps of sharp jelly.

"Shall we go up to Oby's then?" Ruby was walking backwards, gripping a wodge of library books under one arm. They were allowed six for the whole of the holidays and there was still the fortnightly little library at the Mission Hut; plenty to read. Weeks and weeks of reading and messing about and now they'd hooked up with Oby there were loads of reasons to hang around in the Bower Wood.

"What?" Peter had been staring up at the washed-out blue sky, failing to see the skylark that was singing up there somewhere. He was always so pleased when he managed to spot one and kept an account of how many he'd seen over a month.

"See it?" She peered up too, but it didn't count if she was the one to see it and, in any case, it seemed to make Peter feel bad if she did.

"Nah."

"So, shall we, then? Go to the Camp." Ruby loved saying that, it sounded so dark and exciting.

"Today?"

"After tea," Ruby said. The days stretched on, sliding unhurriedly into the summer nights, making time seem wandering and endless, there to be taken.

"Funny he never wants to walk home with us." Peter kicked gently at a hardened ridge left by a tractor, sending up a quick puff of dust.

"It's because of his sister," Ruby sighed. Oby's sister Lily was thought to be too small, at six, to walk with all the Leas' kids and so Oby had a bike with a seat on the back. Anyhow, he'd told Ruby, it was better like that and cut out a lot of the mild bullying that went on between the gypsies and the settled lot.

"Yeah, but this bit, he could cycle with us. Mm?"

Ruby looked at him and then they both laughed. "Not with her, though!" It was true, Lily was wild, a bit like one of the farm cats, go too near and she'd likely as not spit at you, or, worse, scratch your face. In some ways, it was as well Oby took her, otherwise there'd be fights on the way home. As it was, Lily spent a lot of time in the corner when she was at school, or even shut in the paints room, but she wasn't at school that often.

"Come on," Peter said, starting to run, "race you down the hill, first to the egg store wins!"

"That's not fair I'm carrying – " But she began to chase after him. Running was something she was good at.

In the wood

It had been risky, making this little house and on evenings like this, he hardly went inside, but in winter, or during the long darkening November days, in rain and wind, he'd become glad of it, especially during the past few years. Anyway, he was rather satisfied with himself for making such a place, patched together as it was from discarded timber left by the bodgers, the men who lived and worked in another part of the wood, making chairs and simple pieces of furniture. If he'd been a different man, there were many times when he might have approached one of them and asked to work alongside, get back into step with other humans, just to see how it tasted again.

Of course, he could not.

Soon he would walk to the wood's edge, and call for the bird, it was a day or so since he'd last seen her and he was – not worried, exactly – but mildly fretful about her. Clever though she was in the manner of her own kind, she was still vulnerable to other predators, as well as people with guns, some who'd take a shot at anything. He pushed that picture to the back of his thoughts.

He must be careful, though. These warm summer nights meant that others wandered the wood and along its edges; twice in the past few weeks he had almost been seen by some children. One of them he recognised as a gypsy child from the encampment down towards the hop gardens. The other two, a boy and a girl, he surmised to be from the farm and he had a vague recollection of having seen them in the past. Mostly, though, he kept out of sight down there when there were likely to be children around. It was risky enough as it was, when he got the urge to take a midnight wander near the barns and houses. The oast house was safer, being the last place on the track that led to Bower Wood, and it was there he'd found supplies of condensed milk and other tinned stuff that added a welcome variation to his diet of wild offerings.

There! She was roosting high up in this giant spreading cedar tree. He had often wondered how it had come to be here, far from where it belonged, as he was too. Another sort of accident, perhaps. He whistled and for a moment she didn't move. Again and here she was circling down and on to his outstretched arm. It always felt like a kind of miracle.

She shifted slightly and the soft breeze of evening lifted her wing feathers. "Where have you been?" It was a pointless thing to do, but gave him an odd sensation of comfort, he could feel the warmth of her and it was good to be this close to another living creature, one who chose to be there and could lift away at any moment.

"Where?" he repeated, her head swivelled as if she might answer and then she was up and gone, off into the dusky light. But it had been enough to settle his worries. He turned and then changed his mind. Soon it would be dark, no harm then to wander away from the trees for a while, occasionally he needed to feel the freedom of space around him. At this time of day, from the Mound, he should be able to catch a glimpse of the last scraps of sunlight on the distant sea line and imagine the taste of salt on his lips, if he was lucky.

The camp and the wood
"Would she read mine?"

"Maybe." Oby sounded unsure and threw a quick glance at

Ruby's hand as if he'd know from just looking whether it was worthwhile asking his aunt to read Ruby's palm.

The two of them were leaning against the gate watching Nancy pulling at grass tufts, Peter was sharpening a piece of willow ready to make his bow, he'd already made one for Ruby who'd straight away let Oby have a go, who surely could have made his own?

It was the first real day of the holidays and had started hot clear and blue and getting hotter all the time; one good reason, Ruby had argued, for coming up to the camp, where it'd be cooler and maybe they could paddle in the brook, and, anyhow, she wanted to ask Oby something important, that's what she'd said. Full of ideas, as always. Then he'd had to remind her to bring her wings too, which was a bit of a surprise, since she'd been the one who'd gone on and on about trying them out from the big tree on the edge of the wood.

"Is she here?" Ruby could be bossy when she liked, Peter smiled to himself, something Oby'd better get used to.

"Collecting up firewood somewhere." Oby swung down from the gate.

"Firewood? In this weather?"

"Cooking." Peter carried on sharpening, but glanced quickly at Oby to make sure he wasn't embarrassed.

"Oh, sorry." She slid down and went over to him, whispering in his ear, "Wouldn't you like her to read your palm too?"

"Not really." But he was curious and tagged on behind when Oby finally agreed and they went off to find his aunt.

"What d'you think she meant, all that stuff about taking it steady when I tried to fly?"

"Common sense," Peter said, wishing he'd remembered to bring some twine with him so he could finish the bow off properly.

"Oby went all peculiar." Ruby was zig-zagging through the bracken, no real direction in mind.

"Did he?"

She stopped and stared up at him. "Did I do the wrong thing again?" Ever since the business with the swan's feather on her birthday, Ruby was unsure about lots of things she used not to think about much. Now it was all getting more complicated. Even Peter seemed different, more on edge. Was that her fault too?

"He told you it wasn't like fortune telling, not like she was going to tell you exactly what's going to happen and all that." He stopped too and peered ahead, they weren't far from the edge of the wood where the big pine tree stood, it wasn't somewhere they came that often.

Ruby shook her head, it was true, Oby said his aunt didn't read palms much these days and when she did it was mostly to tell people what to watch out for, that was all. And so it had been; they'd ducked into the silty dark of the cooking hut where Oby's aunt was stoking the fire under a big black pot. She'd only stopped for a moment, wiping her own hands on her pinafore before grabbing Ruby's right hand, pulling her out into the light, frowning and then asking: "What do you want to know, little chicken?"

"Er – " It seemed wrong to have to say what she wanted, but she thought for a minute and said, "Will I ever fly? Really, I mean?"

"Oh, you'll fly," she said, laughing a little.

Ruby felt herself tremble. Could it be true?

"I will?" She looked at Peter, but he was as surprised as she was and he held the swan's wings tightly, as if they might just go off on their own after this.

"Not with those!" Oby's aunt laughed again.

"What – ?" Ruby's throat was dry with shock.

"Up there." She jerked her head up to the sky, sharp-patched blue between the tree tops. "But," and she glared hard at Ruby, tightening her grip, "you mind how you go before then."

Yes, that was it, now she remembered. Funny, though, maybe Oby's aunt had meant something else altogether. But what? If Oby had come she'd have asked, it seemed rude to do it where his aunt might hear. Instead he'd been called by his mum to go and watch out for Lily and they knew it meant they should go, calling out that they'd come back tomorrow, most likely.

"Don't worry," Peter told her, privately thinking that you didn't need to be a fortune teller to tell someone to watch out if they were always climbing trees and jumping down to see if they would be able to fly. Any fool knew that.

"Come on." He pushed her gently forwards, "I think it's this way."

And it was as they came into a small clearing they saw him, standing with a bird on his arm, speaking to it like a piece of magic.

The farm

They were up in the attic, Peter sat watching while Ruby rummaged through a box.

"You should have waited!"

"He might have got us." She leant back on her heels, pulling out a small brown leather case, she blew on it and coughed. It hadn't been out of the box for a long time.

"I don't think he saw us." Peter stared out of the window, Ruby's dad was busy in the front garden, it was nearly dark out there, but this was the only chance he had to do anything to his own patch; like everyone on the farm he was busy working on the harvest, and there were still the last of cherries to be picked and he had the hops to look after too. It meant that, mostly, Ruby and Peter could slip about fairly easily and unnoticed, so long as they were back in time for meals.

"You should have let me go back for them anyway."

Ruby stopped what she was doing and looked up at him. "Sorry." He'd taken a lot of trouble to get the wings and then to paint them with his model varnish to stop them ponging and now she'd just left them, lying there in the wood for the Ghost

Man to find, most likely. She shivered at the thought.

"He's not really a ghost, you know," Peter said, still watching Mr. Moon down below, moving gently among his roses, spraying for greenfly.

"How d'you know?" Ruby wanted to believe him, ghosts were a scary idea, she'd never seen one before.

Peter shrugged, "He looked real to me, any case, there's no such thing."

Ruby nodded slowly, but then she remembered, "The bird, though?"

"Falcon," Peter told her, "it was a kestrel, you can train them to do that. Why would a ghost be training a falcon?"

"What's he doing that for?"

"Sort of like a pet – or to catch things, rabbits." Peter pulled his thinking face, dreamy and far-off, working things out, but not in a rush.

She took the camera out of its case and turned it over, there was a film still in there from when she'd been keen on taking photos a couple of years ago. She handed it to Peter.

He looked at it. "Four left, I think. Might not be any good, though, the film. Too old."

"We could try it?" She frowned at him, it was a good idea she was sure, trying to take a photo of the Ghost Man, to prove he existed and they were the ones who'd seen him. Special that was. Beyond that, Ruby couldn't quite fathom why she wanted to do it.

"We could, I s'pose." Peter began fiddling with an old toy her dad had made when Ruby was small, two little wooden men that did a kind of circus twisty act, round and round, when you turned the handle. Always trapped together, going round and round and round.

"Peter! Your mum's calling you." Ruby's mum was shouting up the stairs.

Neither of them said anything, but both knew they wouldn't tell anyone else about who – what – they'd seen in the wood, it was their secret and they needed to uncover it carefully.

"Tomorrow, we'll take some bread and things," Ruby whispered to Peter at the back door. "And the camera," she nodded hard, bossy, the way she was when her mind was made up about things.

"Find your wings too," he reminded her, still sore about them. Had she forgotten? Wasn't she always, always going on about flying and wasn't he the one who wanted to help, who believed it could happen?

"We should tell Oby too?"

"Don't know," Peter whispered back. Not Oby as well, he wanted it to be their secret, Oby – well – Oby was a gypsy and he didn't play games in the same way.

"What are you two whispering about?" Ruby's dad appeared from the shed, carrying a bunch of roses. He pulled one out and gave it to Ruby, "Here, duck, for your bedroom, eh?" It was the nicest he'd been to her since the feather on the fire, so maybe it was all going to be all right again.

"See you," Peter called out as he went through the gap in the hedge between the cottages. "Tomorrow!"

Later, pushing up her window to stare out into the darkness, Ruby looked towards Bower Wood, which in the star-black night seemed to rest on the skyline as if it might be a big sleeping animal, stretched and humped, but only sleeping. Somewhere in the trees was the man they'd seen, who hadn't seen them, that's what Peter reckoned, and tomorrow they'd try and find him again. If he was a ghost then he'd know about flying. Surely?

Ruby sighed and searched her book pile and found one of her favourites about the children who went off and lived by themselves in a barn, wishing she and Peter might do that too – and Oby, yes Oby as well.

The Mound

Up here again, with this longing for sight or smell of the sea. Wanting to escape the echo of that voice, scattering his name like gravel against a window, "Gabriel, Gabriel. I can see you, and you know where to look for me!"

He was beginning to think he might be going mad. Not surprising when he thought about it. All these years with no companion, living on the fringe of life, while everyone else got on with it, work, marriage, family. Family. My God, he ran his fingers though his hair, once black, now streaked with grey, he'd glimpsed himself in the cracked spotted glass that passed for a mirror in the oast house – when was it now? – last winter. It had been a shock to suddenly see his father's face staring back at him in a place he could never be.

His father. Mother. Sister and Anna too, where were they all now? Alive? Who could know and after such terrible times it would be a miracle if they all still lived. He had long since tried to bury all remembrance of them, it was too painful, but now, here they were suddenly on this hill that passed for a shadow of the hills of his home, so clear he stumbled forwards, hands stretched. And then he heard it again.
"Gabriel?"
He tried to imagine the silence back, just the midnight wind rifling through the summer leaves, twisting the stems of the long seedy grasses, creaking the small branches in the hedgerows, that's all.
"Gabriel? Brother?"
"We were never brothers!" He hadn't meant to spit the words out so loudly, but he couldn't stand it. The very idea was appalling. Once – such a far off time now – once he had embraced the notion of brotherhood, standing together sharing everything, laughter, pain, thoughts, ideals, making plans – falling together. No, not that. But in the end it had happened and now he was ashamed to think he could have ever believed in it all. At first, in those early years, he had come across the newspapers left in the oast house, or sometimes blowing in the hedgerows, casually scattering their messages of terrible, almost unimaginable things. But when he read about them it felt right, what he had done and

was another reason why he had never been able to return home.

Now, though, a kind of sickness overcame him, a sharp longing for the places of his childhood, and most of all for the people he had loved. For the first time since it had all happened, fifteen years ago, he began to dance with the thought that perhaps he should try to find his way back again.

"You can never go home." The voice snarled at him. "How will you face them? How will you face yourself?"

"You can't stop me!" He shouted back into the dark. "You bastard! Get away from me! Or, I'll – " Gabriel lifted his fist.

"Or, you'll what?" The old mocking, the half smile, half sneer.

"I'd do it again and again and again." Gabriel's voice was quiet now, iced with the deep, sharp old anger.

"Bastard?" The same sneering. "Me? What about you? Huh, brother? Brother? We both know where it is buried. Huh? Your gun."

"Yes, yes!" Gabriel sank to his knees, not bothering to brush the tears from his face.

And then he saw it, a glow of white drifting in a half circle before landing a short distance away on the other side of the hill. It startled him back to the moment. He held his breath and watched as the swan began to walk awkwardly towards him, how ungainly they were out of their two elements of air and water. He wondered if he should move away, but decided that staying still and quiet was the better thought; it was how he was with her and it seemed to be the best approach.

"What is it you seek?" For it was obvious that the swan would be asking him a question if it could speak, it held its head on one side, enquiring.

And then he remembered.

A month ago he had been on one of his night patrols and he'd found her injured, chest bloodied, she must have flown into something, a power line was the most likely explanation. There was nothing to be done, he could hardly go for help and she did, in truth, seem beyond it. So he wrung her neck in his now long practised way, deciding that her misfortune could become his good luck and provide him with dinner and some more. Carrying her with her stiffening wings, was going to be difficult and so he cut the wings off and, being near the caves, decided to throw them inside out of sight. He had read somewhere that all swans in England were the property of the monarch and it was a crime to kill one. And he had surely enough crimes on his conscience? Silly, perhaps, since who would know, but something about the nobility of this creature demanded this act of secrecy.

Here – her mate, perhaps. Another piece of knowledge came to him. Didn't swans pair for life? The thought suddenly pained him. He squatted as if to seem less threatening to the bird still coming towards him, not that he seemed worried by the man at all.

"Come," Gabriel murmured, holding his hand out to the swan, but for no good reason, having nothing to offer by way of food, not even a scrap of bread. Nothing so civilised. "I mean no harm," he told the swan. It all felt eerie, this glowing white creature coming, still coming, wings spread and moving slightly. For a moment Gabriel half believed that this bird knew that he had been the one who had dispatched his life-long companion, not only that, but he had eaten her too.

Suddenly there was a swirling draught and the swan took off when it was just over an arm's length from where he was. Gabriel had the sensation of having his forehead brushed by feathers, but later he thought he might have imagined this. And it really was the oddest experience because of the other thing that happened afterwards; the swan didn't fly away immediately, but came back over his head three times and the last time a feather fell and landed on Gabriel's shoulder. It seemed, in some fashion, symbolic, but of what he couldn't fathom.

Walking back and later, he twisted the whole experience over in his mind, believing and then dismissing the notion that the swan was the mate of the one he had killed and that it had been a kind of message for him about his own rootless, lonely and uneasy situation. For the moment, though, the voice no longer troubled him.

In the wood

"Ouch! That hurt!" Ruby pushed Peter's arm away.

"Look!" He spoke quietly and pointed. "See?"

Ruby looked down; there between the tangled bracken was a hole, almost hidden, but, luckily for her, not completely. Bower Wood was famous for its wells, one of the reasons they were always being told by all the grown-ups, On no account go wandering too far in, out of sight of the hop garden, all right?

"You were just about to walk right over it," he told her. He didn't sound cross, though, more like his old self again, but he had smiled when they'd called at the camp for Oby and Mrs. Lee said that he'd had to go down to the Stour Wood site with his aunt to see his cousins and that he might be away for a week.

Ruby stopped and peered down the hole, she picked up a stone and chucked it in, they both counted to six before they heard a splash. "Thanks," she said, "you most likely saved my life."

Peter snorted and pushed her again, this time gently, steering her away from the hole. "There's a kind of path," he nodded at the flattened bits of undergrowth, "we should stick to that from now on."

"How come we didn't fall down a well yesterday?" Ruby shivered. "Blimey, that was lucky, eh?"

"Yeah," he agreed, "'spect so."

"You sure we are going the right way, really?"

"Course," he said. "See, there's the big pine."

There, standing much taller than any of the other trees was the pine, it was where they'd been heading for yesterday when they'd seen the man with that bird. Ruby knew she would have to climb this tree, wings or no wings, and she'd get Peter to take a picture of her too, although how they'd get it developed and all without her mum and dad knowing was going to be tricky, but Peter would think of something. He always did.

"Found them!" Peter had run on once they were nearly to the small clearing (and no fear of wells) and now he was holding her wings up and waving them at her.

After several minutes when he'd worked out how he'd fixed them before, Ruby was ready to start climbing. "Don't forget to take the picture," she said, swinging herself up to the first branch. This was usually the hardest part, getting going.

"All right," he shouted, "but don't go too high the first time?"

"I won't!"

He watched as she tried the different branches, stopping every now and then to think about the best way. He'd always been amazed at how she just seemed to know which was going to work and which wasn't, and he liked her pluck too, being scared of heights himself.

"There. That'll do," Ruby said, but too softly for Peter to hear down below. She sat, legs either side of the branch; there was a good view here, not of the sea, although they were now on that side of the wood and if she could ever get to the top – and that'd be the next thing to try for – then, she reckoned she would be able to. Almost as high as the Mound. She swivelled slightly, yes, there it was over the fields and the orchards, almost touchable. She leaned a little towards it.

"Watch it!" Peter's voice trembled up from below.

He looked small and worried and, what's more, he wasn't holding the camera.

"Photo!" she called, but he didn't hear because a sudden breeze lifted her words and tossed them up into the blue sky.

Oh, well, she could climb up again. She looked at the ground, the best landing spot was on the other side away from Peter, the trees were really thinning out there where the field's edge began.

It was as she started to jump, flapping her wings to catch the breeze, it was then she saw him, shocked and white-faced, appearing suddenly from further along the wood's fringe. The man, Ghost Man, waving his arms and he was shouting something. It was hard to hear and his words sounded sharp and tight, but one of them sounded like Angel.

Perhaps it was that which made her wobble. But by then it was too late. Next she heard Peter shouting to the man, telling him to Get out of the bloody way!

Hidden in the grass was one of the huge number of flint stones that littered the farm, it must have been one of those she caught her head on, Peter reckoned afterwards. Whatever it was, it changed everything.

The farm

Peter pushed open the door and eased himself into the darkness of the oast house. His breath, coming as it was in huge gasping gulps sounded as loud as a train in the soft muffled stillness and he took in great mouthfuls of the oily, hop-musky tasting air. He knew what to look for because he and Ruby played here all the time – as much as they could get away with – during hop-picking. And, anyway, the man had shouted it at him.

"The box, with the cross on, yes?"

Peter had nodded, too shocked to speak.

"You must bring it. Now!" The man had barked at him and so he'd run, leaving his already blood-stained handkerchief as a make-shift bandage until he returned.

"And," the man had pulled him sharply by his collar, "tell no one. You understand?"

Again, Peter had nodded, afraid now. The man looked wild and fearsome, with black hair straggling to his shoulders, and that voice all sharp and angry sounding.

"Be fast! I shall stay here with her!"

It was strange, being in here when it wasn't hop-picking time, they were always being told Don't mess about in the oast on your own! Although sometimes they ignored that one, always taking care not to touch any of the machinery or tread on the hop pockets, or muck about in any of the places that were out of bounds at all times. But now, Peter stood for a moment, trying to remember where the box was kept; the man had said something, but in the hectic pounding run from the far side of the woods, down the track, across the railway bridge, on, on down the lane to the farmyard, it had got silted up with the panic of it all.

The bunk room, perhaps? It was where he and Ruby would go with their books, taking it in turns to try out the different beds and dipping their fingers into the sweet condensed milk, always open on the table for the men to put in their tea. He searched all the likely places in there, but couldn't see it at first and then, just as he was about to go and try upstairs, he noticed a black box, half covered with sacking on one of the chairs. Stencilled on the lid was a bright red cross. Peter grabbed it and then almost dropped it as someone called out.

"Who's that?"

He held his breath, convinced that whoever it was would hear his heart beating, so loud it thudded in his ears. Peter shifted as quietly as he could, easing himself behind the door, hoping it would be enough.

"Charlie?" It was Stan, looking for Ruby's dad. Peter knew he'd have to start breathing soon, otherwise he might burst. "That you in there?"

Peter could hear him, any second he'd be in the bunk room and there was no time to roll into hiding in one of the spaces underneath the bottom bunks, because he'd be seen for sure. On tiptoes he was ready to run.

Stan was already through the door. "Peter?"

"Mr. Pierce." He shuffled the box behind him, but too late, Stan had already spotted that too.

"What's this?" He waved at the First Aid box, which had started to come open, a bandage – just what he needed! – unravelling itself in the space between them both.

Stan pushed his cap back on his head, which made him seem more like a ferret than ever, Peter decided. He never felt quite easy with him, it was as if Stan expected kids to be trouble before they'd had a chance to prove otherwise. And Peter had once felt the sharp back of his hand when he'd been grabbing a handful of cherries that he'd just picked. No, Stan could only ever be Stan behind his back to him and Ruby, it was always Mr. Pierce to his face.

"You'll catch it when I tell Charlie you're in here thieving the medical box." He jabbed a finger too near to Peter's eye. "Eh? What do you think he's going to say to that?" He flicked a glance out into the main body of the oast then, as if remembering something. "On your own, are you?"

Peter started to wonder if he'd ever be able to talk again. It had been a day of shocks so far and now he didn't know what to do or say. All that was racing through his head was that he had to get this box to Ruby and the man, that Ruby could be bleeding to death for all he knew and if she was it would be his fault. He understood now, in some corner of his mind, that Stan was somehow more scary than the man and he didn't know why he knew this.

"A game," Peter finally stuttered, "we were just borrowing it for a minute."

Stan leaned against the table and smiled nastily. "Oh, yeah?"

"Ruby's – " He tried to think, ah yes that would do, "Ruby's dad said it was all right, so long as we brought it back straight after we'd finished." Peter wasn't used to lying and he felt his face heating up.

"Did he now?" Stan stayed where he was, one hand scratching at his greasy hair as if the truth might appear.

"Yes." Peter straightened up, near enough to the door to slip out and make a run for it; he hoped Stan had left the outside door open. He started to roll the bandage up and clamp the box lid shut with one hand.

"So, where's she, then?" Stan smirked.

"Er – round the back," Peter stumbled, "in the lean-to." There was a small shed behind the oast, where he and Ruby once made a camp from the old straw bales that got dumped in there if there wasn't room on the trailer. Everyone knew about it and mostly left them to it. Peter was banking on Stan believing this part of the story and letting him go right away.

"Funny, I just came by there and didn't see her." Then, as if he had all the time in the world, he drew his tobacco tin from his pocket and then fished around in the other for his Rizlas.

Peter took his chance then and ran.

In the wood

When Ruby opened her eyes she saw him: the Ghost Man, staring down at her, a brown face, with deep brown eyes, and creases everywhere as he frowned. He was muttering at her too, only none of it made sense. She felt her own eyes folding back shut, but he shook her quite firmly.

"Do not sleep now!" Cor, that was better, she got what he was saying this time.

"Happened?" was all she could manage.

"The tree, you fell." He moved her head very gently placing something soft underneath. It felt better being able to rest her neck properly, but now she was feeling another pain. Her arm; Ruby shifted it slightly. "Ouch!"

"It might have broken," the man was crouching next to her, touching her elbow. "When you landed on the ground."

Ruby wasn't sure what that would mean. Mum and Dad were going to be cross, that was certain, her mum was always telling her to be careful with all this jumping off things. She pictured Dad having to take her down to the doctor in the village; Doctor Bertram. He'd most likely be cross too and tell her she was a silly girl, he'd said the same thing when she was five and had nearly died of pneumonia.

"What were you doing, so high up?" The man nodded his head up at the tree. He lifted her wings, which had got squashed and bent, with a few of the feathers coming loose. "Like a bird? Huh?" He was smiling now and when he did he definitely seemed much less scary.

"Like a bird," she repeated staring at him. His voice was funny, sharp, making her think of a dog's soft growl. "Are they broken too?" She meant the wings.

He held them up and turned them over carefully in his hands, smoothing the ruffled feathers. "Not as bad as your arm," he said, smiling again. "It would be possible to make them better very fast, I think it – " He lifted his head. There was a noise getting closer, someone crashing fast through the undergrowth. The man stood and peered into the deeper darkness of the wood, frowning now.

"Found it – " Peter was suddenly there, breathing in quick, harsh gasps, holding the box Ruby remembered from the oast bunk room. It gave her a strange feeling seeing it here, completely out of its place.

"You are a good boy," the man told Peter, setting the box down beside him and sorting through it quickly but without fussing. "Ah, here," he pulled out a bottle of antiseptic and unscrewed the top, sniffing it, then he examined the label. "Yes, yes," he was saying half to himself now, "this is what will do the task." He rifled in the box some more and unpacked some lint, pouring antiseptic on he gave Ruby a serious look. "This will – er – " he seemed to be searching for the word.

"Sting," Peter said, helpful as always, kneeling down next to her too.

"That is correct," the man agreed, "but it will also be helpful for the germs. To kill them," he added, seeing Ruby's anxious face. "I shall lift your head now, do not be afraid."

Peter caught hold of her hand and squeezed it while the man moved Ruby's head forwards ever so slightly and then pressed the thick piece of lint doused in antiseptic on to a place just above her neck. She winced for a moment and thought she might cry, but Peter was holding tight and she didn't want to let him down.

"Now," the man searched the box again and found some sticking plaster, he measured a strip and then cut it quickly from a knife that he suddenly produced from out of one of his pockets. Peter let go of Ruby's hand for a minute, shocked by the sight of the Ghost Man holding this glinty bit of danger. The man seemed not to have noticed this and handed the roll to Peter, "Put this back, yes?" Peter nodded and did as he was told, his breath catching in his throat as thoughts started to come clearer in his mind.

"Ah," now the man was pulling at the roll of bandage that Peter had stuffed untidily back into its packet when he'd run from the oast. He wondered if he was going to bandage Ruby's head, or what he might be going to use it for. "Will you help, please?" He looked across at Peter, who struggled to make the words boiling away inside come out properly.

"What do you want me to do?"

"Like this," and the man showed him how to support Ruby's back, so that she could lean forwards and be supported while he made a sling for her arm.

"There," he said, when they were done, "it is not too tight, no?" He was leaning back on his haunches and frowning at her. During the whole process Ruby had kept quiet only now and then looking at Peter to make sure he wasn't going to run off and leave her.

"How does it feel, Ruby?" Peter whispered.

"It's all right," she managed, but now the tears did come.

"You must drink now," the man said and lifted her gently. "Come. Follow me." He jerked his head at Peter.

The hut in the wood

Ruby slept for a long time after she had drunk two cups of thick sweet tea from the tin mug. It tasted just like oast house tea, mostly because of the condensed milk, except there was a smokier shadow to it from the fire the water had been heated over.

Peter watched and said very little, but taking notice of all the things the man had stashed away in this tiny hut. Lots of them were recognisable from the rumours and gossipings of missing items from the farm and other places; there was the big black cooking pot from the cookhouse near the hopper huts down by the Dane Acres hop garden, everyone had reckoned that was definitely the gypsies; a stash of tins too, from the huts and, most probably, the oast. Lots of stuff like this was easily found around the farm, left there for when people were working too far from the cottages to nip back for tea or dinner; there was even an iron bedstead put to use here so that the man had a proper bed to sleep on and a pile of sacks and pokes as make-shift blankets; books too (where from? that was a mystery), and piles and piles of newspapers, some faded and yellow; nets too, for trapping, Peter knew that, and several sizes of catapult too; the gun was propped in the corner near the door and, he noticed, several boxes of cartridges, obviously the ones that Stan Pierce's mum had been on about to Mr. Harris, that time in the shop. How long ago that seemed now. All that talk of the Ghost Man and here they were, in his hut, Ruby sleeping on the bed, the man busy gathering what looked like vegetables from an old apple box, while the water still bubbled in the pot over the fire. Was he going to poison them now, Peter wondered dreamily, or make some spell and then cook them, like the witch in the fairy story. Perhaps the water was for them? I must keep awake, he thought, I must, in case – but what with the scent of the wood smoke filling the small space on top of everything else that had happened already that day, he too was soon asleep.

"Here, you must eat." Peter felt himself being shaken and when he opened his eyes he was afraid, not understanding at first, where he was. "Soup," the man was bending over him. He blinked and sat up. "Here," the man said again, handing him a wooden spoon and a beaten old tin bowl full of steaming and rich smelling vegetable stew. Peter glanced over at Ruby, still spark out on the bed, the man didn't try and wake her.

"She must rest, yes?" he said, as if guessing what Peter was thinking. "After a shock it is the best thing to do." And he too began to eat the stew, quickly and hungrily and without keeling over in a poisoned fit, so Peter did the same and once he started couldn't stop until he was finished. It was like nothing he'd ever tasted before, which was strange because it seemed to be made from all the things his dad grew in their garden, but this had something else too, something that made it rich, sharp and herby, moreish, his dad would say.

"More?" The man was smiling at him, Peter saw now for the first time, that one of his front teeth was missing. He nodded, trying not to stare. "My name is Gabriel," the man told him. "And you?"

"Me?"

"My name is Gabriel." He pointed at his chest.

"Oh, Peter."

"Apieter?" Gabriel frowned.

"Peter," Peter said again.

"Ah, of course," Gabriel smiled, "Peter!" He held out his hand, "Yes?" he encouraged.

"Sorry," Peter mumbled, it felt like a very grown-up thing to be doing, shaking hands and a bit peculiar too, here in the middle of Bower Wood in a hut he'd never known was here until today and with a man called Gabriel who didn't sound as if he was from these parts. But he didn't feel much like a ghost either, judging by the rough strength of his hands and the hot, steamy realness of his stew.

They were quiet again for a few minutes while they both ate some more and in the quietness, Peter could hear the soft snores of Ruby as she slept on, and outside nearby a robin was singing. Gabriel cocked his head, "Listen, yes?"

"A robin," Peter said, wondering if maybe the man didn't know, being from London, or somewhere perhaps.

"He is one of my friends," Gabriel explained and Peter could see by his serious look that he really did mean it. "Until you," he waved at Ruby too, "I – well – I do not see many people." Something obviously came to him then, and he frowned. "It will be important, this thing I must ask you."

Peter sat still and stiff, it sounded worrying. "What?"

"When you and Ruby go home would you please not to tell about me and where I live?"

"I – er – " Peter hadn't thought about that, well, he hadn't thought about much since it had all happened, and he'd had to find the First Aid box, get away from Stan, come back as fast as he could because Ruby might be killed for all he knew. And now, it dawned on him; they'd have to go home eventually, 'course they would, how daft he was being. It had all seemed like it belonged somewhere else until the man, Gabriel, had said that. Worse than that, he suddenly understood, they were going to have to explain about Ruby and what had happened and all the business with the box. Stan was most likely already blabbing about it. Blimey! Peter looked at his watch.

"S'nearly five o'clock," he blurted.

"I thought it might be," Gabriel answered, peering out into the watered green light of the wood. Didn't seem as if he had a watch, then.

"We must go home." Peter stood up, handing Gabriel his empty bowl. "Thanks, it was good stew."

"You are welcome." Gabriel gave a slight bow, which made Peter want to laugh. "But first, we must wake Ruby and she must eat too."

Unlike Peter, Ruby wasn't so hungry, more thirsty than anything, which meant that Gabriel had to go outside and draw up more water from one of the wells that he used for his needs.

"We have to go soon, Ruby." Peter looked at her, not sure how they were going to do any of this. Could she walk? He wasn't sure and it really was quite a long way all of a sudden. And as it was, this was the furthest they'd ever been in the wood, nearly to the other side, well away from Bower farm land. His legs felt heavy.

"Yes," she said, staring at him big-eyed and a bit white and pasty-faced. Was she going to be sick?

Gabriel ducked back in with a mug of water and she drank it down in one go hardly taking a breath. "I shall bring more?"

She nodded, wiping her mouth with the sleeve of her good arm. "It's got brown stuff in it."

"It will not harm you."

"Tastes all right, though," she said.

"You going to be able to walk?" Peter asked.

"Yes, silly," she rolled her eyes at him, "it's me arm that's hurt."

"I know, but," he chewed his lip, because there were other worries pinching at him too, "what are we going to tell them at home? Your dad's going to be really cross."

Ruby frowned, "What d'you mean?"

"We're going to get into trouble, me especially."

"I'll just say," she thought for a minute or two, licking her lips, still thirsty and flicking a look towards the opening, wondering where Gabriel had got to. "I fell out of a tree with my wings, I'm always jumping aren't I? No one's going to know about – " She waited for Peter to say the right thing, like he always did.

"We'll have to think of something." He started mooching about, which was awkward in the small, dark space of the hut. They'd have to get their story right otherwise they might not be allowed up here again and the wood was one of their best places.

Gabriel came back with more water and then helped Ruby to stand up. "I feel dizzy," she said as if it might be someone's fault.

"You must walk around for a little," Gabriel said, "outside. Come." He held out his hand and signalled to Peter that he must come too. "Try and see how you feel. Better now," he took some deep breaths to show Ruby that she must do the same.

"Come on, Ruby," Peter put a hand on her shoulder, because it looked as if she might cry any minute and her face was even whiter than before.

"It hurts!"

Peter looked at Gabriel and then cleared his throat. "I'm sorry Mister but – " He stopped.

"You will need help, yes? I must carry her." He squatted down in front of Ruby and touched her lightly on the injured arm. "Do not be afraid, I shall try not to hurt you, but you must – let me see – yes, trust me. You understand?"

Ruby's face went tight and she nodded. Peter knew that she most likely was afraid, but she was trying to be brave. He'd seen that expression in the past when she was choosing to try an especially difficult and high jump from a tree she'd never jumped from before. He bent down to her too and whispered, "I've said I'll help, don't worry, eh?"

Ruby nodded again and swallowed hard. "I'll be all right." She stared at Gabriel. "Ready," she said.

Once she was as comfortable as she could be, they moved quickly through the wood and, at times, Peter had to hurry to keep up. His legs, he soon realised, were feeling heavy and slow after the hectic run he'd had to make from the oast and Stan. It seemed much further this time. He'd be glad to get back home.

It was as they got near to Oby's camp that Gabriel suddenly stopped and called over his shoulder, "Is there someone here who could take you back to the farm, eh?"

"I, er – " Peter peered through the thinning trees below them and saw a thin curl of smoke rising from the cookhouse chimney, smelt the familiar sharp woodiness of it. If Oby was there it'd be a lot easier, somehow it felt harder to go into the camp without him. "Our friend, Oby, has gone to visit – " and just as he was about to finish he saw Oby coming from the place where the white goat was tethered. Without thinking he ran forwards, lifted his hand and called out.

Behind him now, Gabriel muttered something he didn't quite catch, but he sounded cross. He stopped and lowered Ruby to the ground. "I am sorry, Peter," he said, more gently this time, "I do not wish that others see me. Remember, what I told you?"

Peter frowned up at him. Wasn't he going to take Ruby all the way home, then? How was he going to manage? There was still nearly a mile to go, by his reckoning. Supposing Oby couldn't – or wouldn't – help. Then what? He lifted his arms as if to say all this. Ruby, propped carefully against a tree trunk had gone that papery white colour again and she seemed to be having trouble keeping her eyes open. "What's matter?" she said.

"I must go, Little Miss," Gabriel explained, touching the top of her head. "Peter and your friends from the gypsies will get you home. It will be well. I think perhaps your arm is not broken." He smiled. "I shall say goodbye."

"Don't go," Ruby whispered, awake from the fear of being left, the tears coming fast now and soon turning to sobs. "Please, Mr. Gabriel, can't you just take me home? Please?"

"S' all right Ruby," Peter told her, not believing it, "we'll manage. Gabriel has to go, remember we mustn't tell. It's a secret?"

Caught up by this strange moment of parting, none of them had heard Oby arrive, clever as he was at moving fast and quietly. He stood for a moment, staring at the three of them, taking it all in as best he could. So, this was the Man they had seen moving like a shadow in the wood, here he was, not a ghost at all, he must tell his aunt.

"Hello, Ruby, Peter?" He knelt next to Ruby and touched her arm. "What happened?"

No one answered for a minute; even Gabriel, who had been about to leave, just stood very still, as if not moving might help solve this new problem. "I must go," he said half to himself, but making no attempt to. It was as if Oby's arrival had tangled them all in a spell.

"She fell out of a tree," Peter began to explain, and then out it all came in a great gush, every detail so clear that Ruby had opened her eyes wide and still Gabriel stayed where he was, resting one of his hands flat against the tree trunk, as if he might be afraid it was going to topple over on them. His face creased and serious, and his eyes fixed on Oby all the time Peter was spilling out the story.

"I thought you weren't supposed to be here," Peter said, finally.

"Lily's staying at Aunty Mina's instead." Oby shrugged. It was the way things always were with Oby and his family, nothing ever seemed fixed down properly, even ordinary things like who was staying where. Peter couldn't get the hang of it.

"It's hurting," Ruby whined, "and my bum's sore and the ants are getting too close, look." A group of wood ants was beginning to investigate a fallen piece of branch next to her good arm, climbing over and marching along as if on an expedition of their own.

Peter checked his watch, "Bloody hell, we got to go." He looked at Gabriel.

"You will help them," Gabriel told Oby.

"My dad isn't back yet." Like lots of other people from the site, Oby's dad was busy with the last of the cherry picking. He had an old green Austin van and would have been able to take Ruby home in a few minutes, but walking was going to be difficult, Peter and Oby were both quite skinny and Ruby needed careful carrying by the looks of it.

"You must go now," Gabriel said, his voice hard and ragged. He put his hands on Peter's shoulders. "Tell your friend what I have asked, yes? I do not wish to be seen."

Peter wondered why he didn't tell Oby himself, but he nodded quickly, "Promise," he said. It was as if Gabriel, like them, might get into trouble with the grown-ups and needed the same kind of protection as any other of their friends. Suddenly, Gabriel moved, walking off so fast that within seconds he could have been just another shifting pattern caught somewhere between light and dark as the late afternoon sun fingered its way between the tree tops.

The farm

It had been Peter's idea to use Oby's bodge to carry Ruby like some battered fairy queen back down the track to the farm. It was just right, if a bit bumpy, made from an old wooden coal scuttle dumped at the tip, below the bomb hole. Oby had found some pram wheels and fixed a plank of wood and tied hop string to help with steering. It had won a couple of bodge races up on the Mound, when Oby could be bothered to join in, mostly he used it to whiz down the steep bank of the bomb hole, where he'd made a smooth path good for speed.

"You all right?" Peter was worried, Ruby looked ever so pale again and suddenly the farm seemed miles away.

"Bit tired." She yawned then and shifted slightly. They'd padded out the bodge with some cushions from Oby's caravan, but he'd had to fetch them without being seen. They all decided without saying anything, that it was best to involve as few people as possible. It was going to be bad enough explaining all this to Ruby's mum and dad.

"I'll steer 'til we get to the huts," Oby said, "yes?" He blinked his quick dark eyes at Peter who nodded. The hopper huts were about half way down the track, you could see the oast from there and, tipped on the top of the skyline, the roofs of the cottages. Maybe it wouldn't take so long after all.

Just as they set off Peter thought he saw someone on the edge of the hop garden, he'd felt eyes staring at them; but when he looked again whoever, or whatever it was had darted out of sight. He wondered if it was the man, Gabriel, but then realised it couldn't be because they'd watched him stride off back into the shifting, whispered shadowed green of the wood, heading for his hut. There was no reason for him to be on the side of the track. No, it wasn't him, yet there was something familiar in the movement.

"You coming?" Oby had already started pushing and trying to steer the bodge at the same time, quickly finding out that it was going to take forever like that.

"I'll pull while you push," Peter said, taking care not to offend Oby who could be touchy at times, especially about his things and his ideas.

So, off they went taking nearly half an hour to get down to the farmyard, which normally took them ten minutes, less if they ran. Meanwhile, the figure that had been watching them from the edge of the hop garden, now turned his attention to a much more interesting question. The identity of that bloke who'd appeared out of the wood with the kids, like some bloody tramp. No, that wasn't quite right, although he was dressed in rough and ready clothes, and his hair was long, pulled back in some poncy ponytail, he didn't move the way tramps move. He seemed, well, almost too sure of himself, cocky. Might be worth a look, then. He'd spotted the path and figured if he got a move on he might catch him up.

Once Ruby was in bed and after the doctor had gone, Peter was called round to explain himself. He'd had his tea and Oby, although invited in by Peter's mum had said, No, he had to get home, but thank you.

"Polite lad," Peter's dad remarked, sitting down and unfolding his paper. Nodding to himself, "I've always said so."

Peter wondered, Said so to who? But he didn't ask, he was saving his breath for the story he was going to have tell next door, at the Moons'.

"Now, then Peter, what exactly happened?" They'd asked him to come and sit in the front room, where it felt too quiet and tidy, he'd have preferred the kitchen with its big square, scrubbed table, where sometimes he and Ruby played table tennis on wet days, making sure not to hit the ball into the range, where it'd have melted for sure. As it was, this was strange, everything seemed muffled and heavy, with just the round brown-framed clock on the mantle giving off its slow, serious tick.

"A tree," Peter began, sitting right on the edge of the sofa, afraid of sinking back and never being able to leave, without first telling everything that had happened.

"A tree," Ruby's dad repeated and he sighed. "Ruby and her bloody climbing." He threw a look at Mrs Moon as if it might be her fault.

"It's because of the wings," Peter licked his dry lips, "that I'd made for her."

"Oh, those swan's wings?" Ruby's mum said it like a question, but she knew really, because Ruby had got her to find some strong thread from the sewing basket, to help tie them on tighter.

"Sorry." He wondered if that might be enough, that if he took the blame they'd not ask for too many details because they could just be cross with him; it was often how things worked, he'd found, when he and Ruby got up to mischief, as it was often called. If one of them took the blame – and it was usually him! – then that could be the end of it.

Not this time.

"Let me get this straight," Mr. Moon gave him a hard stare, "she jumped out of a tree flapping those bloody wings, thinking she'd fly. Did you encourage her?"

"Charlie." Mrs Moon, leant across and touched Ruby's dad's arm, as if he might be a dog getting over-excited, but he shook it off.

"Did you?"

"Well, um – "

"Calm down Charlie." Ruby's mum appealed, trying to give Peter a reassuring smile.

"I didn't tell her not to." Which was about as true as it could be and everyone knew that telling Ruby not to climb and not to jump out of trees, was useless anyway, she was always up and then in the air before you could stop her. And, besides, Peter, hating heights like he did, generally stood back and watched. What else was he supposed to do?

"No, well." Ruby's dad leaned back and Peter took a breath.

There was something else he had tell them too, because they'd all hear about it soon enough from Mr. Pierce. "I came back for the First Aid box, to the oast," he added unnecessarily.

"What?"

"The First Aid box," he repeated, "but I've put it back now, so it's all right. I just used the bandage, you know, to help with Ruby's arm."

Mr. Moon made a phoof noise and shook his head in disbelief.

"You did what you thought was right, Peter, eh?" Ruby's mum was being much more understanding about it all.

"Ruby's got a bloody broken arm!" Mr. Moon shouted, "She's going to have to go the hospital tomorrow, to have it properly set" (it was true, Doctor Bertram had put a temporary splint on, they'd said, he thought it was a clean break and a good night's rest in her own bed was probably for the best) "and the boy farts around with a bandage instead of coming to find someone. Bloody what-me!"

Peter shifted in the chair, wondering if it would be all right for him to go in a minute. He'd told them the important bits. Well, all they were going to hear from him, anyway. Was Ruby going to be able to keep quiet about the man – Gabriel? It was going to be hard to explain that one. But he sensed she would somehow. He'd made it sound important, more important than anything else, keeping his presence in the wood a secret. Gabriel had been kind to them too, just giving the help that was needed without accusing him, or Ruby, of being in the wrong. It was as if he was one of them, older and better able to cope with people falling out of trees and breaking their arms. He hadn't treated them as if they were kids, and it was like he really cared about them, making them soup and all that. No, they mustn't know about Gabriel. Never. Not from him.

"Peter?" Ruby's mum was kneeling in front of him. "You're tired, time to go home and go to bed I think. Come on." She grabbed his hands and pulled him gently up.

"One more thing." Mr. Moon started.

"Charlie." Ruby's mum sounded disappointed.

"No, no – just young Oby Lee that's all. Was he mixed up in

all this?"

Peter shook his head. "He just helped bring her back, on his bodge, I mean. That's all. Sorry."

"Humph. Yes, well, keep away from the woods from now on. All right?"

Peter nodded, telling himself that a nod didn't really count as a promise. Did it?

In the wood

He sat outside his hut staring up at the star-packed sky and breathing in the sharp familiar sweetness of the night air. For the first time in a long while he had craved a draw or two on his pipe. It was an old clay thing he'd come across when digging in the woods, just a chip off the end of the stem, but otherwise serviceable and he'd found some herbs that he recognised from the forest of his youth and ground them into a fairly pleasing substitute for the tobacco he remembered smoking so long ago. Next time he was near the oast house perhaps he'd go in and see if one of the workers had left any tobacco around. He'd done it before. But.

Gabriel let the whisper of smoke free from the corner of his mouth and watched as it disappeared into the darkness. A shift of breeze stirred the leaves, as if someone had just run their hand across the tree tops, otherwise all was quiet, not even the little owl calling now from where, earlier, it had been hunting down by the stream at the wood's edge. The children, how glad of their sudden unexpected company he'd been and yet saddened by it too. Now that contact had been formed it would be difficult to break and difficult for the children to keep his secret. No matter how much they meant to one day they would tell someone, or just by knowing themselves, accidentally reveal him and the life that, until now, he had been able to live on the fringes of the world. And it had been good, for the most part, while it had lasted. He had known that one day he would have to decide again, whether to stay or go. Only this time, no one would have to die in the cause of his choice.

It wasn't only the children, though; it was the watcher, the one who had started to haunt his steps. Even this afternoon, as he was moving back into the safety of the tree cover, he could feel that he was being observed, not just the farewell waves and glances from Ruby, Peter and – what was he called, the gypsy boy, Obadiah? – no, it was more than their harmless stares. Gabriel had seen the figure of a man, a muffled shape, no more, in the shade of the thick weight of bines, standing at the end of one of the rows of the hop garden. Definitely watching him, he had sensed the eyes at his back for a long while as he took one of his carefully planned diversionary paths back towards his hut. Once he'd stopped and spun swiftly round to try and catch a proper look, he'd even been about to call out the name he hadn't spoken for many years, but the clumsy crashings of a pheasant nearby had brought him back to earth.

Tonight, though, he held a sense of peace about him, no watching eyes, no whispers of his name, just the soft calm that steadied his normal wary fretting. Nights like this, sitting here with his pipe, he was at ease and, with sudden shock, he understood that he was also at home.

It was going to be a hard thing to leave now.

The Leas

Ruby and Peter were sitting on the grass bank across the road from The Half Moon, both their dads were inside washing away the dust of the corn harvest with their usual Friday night pints. Peter was holding a bottle of ginger beer for Ruby while she finished off the chips bought from the Fish and Chip Man who came every Friday to this part of the Leas. It had been a week now, since she'd had the plaster put on, with another five to go, the doctor had told her mum and dad. "The whole holiday!"

Ruby had moaned. "It's not fair!" Her dad had told her that she might think of that the next time she thought she could go jumping out of trees and nearly killing herself, eh?

"What did Oby say?" Ruby squinted at Peter who was holding up the bottle to the light and watching the bubbles rise and fall.

"About what?" He wondered if Ruby would offer him the last chip like she usually did.

"Mr. Gabriel." She passed the greasy bag across to him, and he passed her the bottle, positioning the straw so she could drink.

"It's not Mister, Gabriel's his first name," Peter ate the last chip, screwed the bag into a tight ball and hurled it towards the bin.

"What'd he say, any case?" She slurped some more and then burped. "Sorry," she giggled and offered Peter the bottle.

"Hasn't seen him, he says. Not since last week, when we – you know." Peter shrugged and took a swig of the ginger beer.

"Dad's told me we're not allowed." Ruby sighed.

"So's mine," Peter said.

"But, still," she nudged him with her good arm.

"Yeah." He nudged her back.

"Come, on give us a hand up, let's go and ask for another bottle."

Inside their dads were playing darts with some of the other blokes from the village, so they hung back by the door, waiting for a minute. Coming in from the last bright glimmers of the summer's evening, it took a moment to adjust their eyes and they didn't notice Stan sitting there next to them until he spoke.

"Some game, then?" He nodded at Ruby's plaster.

"It was my fault," Peter said in a panic, hoping he could stop any more questions by wrongly taking the blame.

"S'not what I heard," Stan took his time, taking a long draw on his roll-up before tilting his head back and letting the smoke curl up towards the yellowed ceiling, rather like the shadow of a snake.

"No, it was me." Even though Ruby had never liked Stan, she tried smiling at him and she could look sweet when she wanted to. "I fell out of a tree," she shrugged, "should've been more careful."

Stan twisted his nose into a sneer. "Should be more careful who you get mixed up with, you mean?"

"Oby was helping," Ruby explained. She'd heard some people on the farm mutter about him after that night, when he and Peter had hauled her back through the yard like some ragged-looking princess in a roughly-made carriage. They'd straight away thought Oby had done something wrong, quick to lay blame on him and his kind.

"I didn't mean the gyppo," Stan said, staring hard at Peter and stubbing his dog-end hard into the already full ashtray.

"Come on Rubes," Peter pulled his eyes away from Stan's and shoved her in the back, "let's go and ask our dads for another drink." But Stan grabbed him by the sleeve.

"You be careful son, eh? Never know what could happen in those woods."

It was one of those moments like watching a plate that has somehow become balanced too near to the edge of a table, you know it's going to fall and break, but can't put out a hand to stop and so, down it goes. Peter should have pulled away without answering, but he didn't.

"What do you mean?"

There was a stillness.

"That bloke," Stan's breath was sharp with the stale tang of fags and beer.

"Bloke?" Peter jumped.

"In the woods, living there, I shouldn't wonder, by the looks of him. The one who thieves from us, him."

"I don't know – "

"Come on." Ruby tugged at him. They had to get away from Stan, the look in his eyes made her shiver.

"Listen, boy." Stan still had him by the sleeve, but at just below table height so no one casually glancing their way would notice. "Listen, you stay away from him, he's dangerous. You and your little girl friend and the gyppo, if you get my meaning. Otherwise I shall have to be telling Charlie and your dad, then you'll be in serious trouble."

"Ye-es." Peter hadn't meant to say that, he hadn't meant to speak at all.

Suddenly Stan let go of him, yet he couldn't move, not straight away. "I'll sort him out, oh yes, just wait." This more to himself than to the kids, his eyes hard and staring at something not there.

"Peter." Ruby sounded scared and Peter followed her through the knot of men at the bar and over to the darts mat.

Back outside, on the bank they sat drinking without talking, struck into silence, as the weight of Stan's words sank in, until Ruby said she felt like having a go on the swings and would Peter give her a hand.

"See that?" He pointed up into the soft deepening blue of the evening sky.

"What?" Ruby leaned back, her arms hooked where he'd placed them round the chains of the swing, she squinted at the end of his finger. "S'bright," she said.

"Jupiter," Peter told her. He knew these things.

"Pretty," Ruby said and wondered if Gabriel could see it too from his hut in the woods.

"I'm going tomorrow," Peter spoke so quietly she almost didn't hear. "We have to tell him." He twisted round and looked down at her.

"Yes," she said, "but I'm coming too."

The farm

Mum was busy frying up some bits of beef for a stew later and saying something about tidying. Ruby was standing at the open back door, waiting for Peter. He was late. They had planned it last night; allowed out for just a bit longer, they'd sat on the fat branch of the old pine on the bank across the road from the cottages and decided they'd say they were going to the Mound for a picnic and they'd most likely stay all day. It was a favourite place for Ruby, everyone knew that, because you could see the farm and – on the distant lick of skyline – the sea too, when it was clear like today was going to be. Only, they weren't going to the Mound, but to Bower Wood. They had to see Gabriel and warn him about Stan.

"He gives me the creeps," Peter said. It was unusual for him to be worried by people, but Stan worried him.

"Me too," Ruby agreed, although truthfully, she'd never had much to do with him until now. He was always there, but in the background, lurking and trying to keep on the right side of her dad who was the Oast Manager. And she'd heard her dad say that Stan wanted to work in there this year, but he wasn't so sure. There was a reason for this, but only Ruby's mum knew what it was.

"Did you hear?" her mum was asking now.

"My bedroom," Ruby murmured.

"This afternoon, so I want you to tidy your room, eh? Best you can, anyway, I'll help when I've done here."

"But I was – we were going to the Mound, for our picnic, me and Peter."

"Well, you'll have to go another day, plenty more days, eh?"

Ruby sighed, it was bad enough not being able to climb her favourite places at the moment, the picnic was supposed to be a way of making up for all that. Now look.

So when Peter finally arrived with grease-proof bags carrying the sandwiches he'd made, she took him upstairs telling her mum he'd help with the tidying, All right?

"I'll have to go on my own," he said, sitting on the bed watching as she cack-handedly moved a pile of books off the window sill.

64

"No, we've both got to go, I've had an idea," Ruby told him.

"I don't see why," Peter got up and helped stack some of the books into the bookcase. "And to be honest, Rubes, it'll be quicker if I go on my own."

They both knew he was right, although she was getting used to the plaster, the weight of it and the aches did make her tired more quickly than normal. "I need to," she said, frowning at him to make sure he understood. He recognised that look. He sighed, no point in arguing

"What's your idea then?"

"We just go later, that's all. When we're done here."

"There won't be enough time, before it gets dark, I mean, we have to get back. Gabriel's hut – "

She glanced over her shoulder at the closed door, "Shush."

"Gabriel's hut," he whispered, "is right over the other side of the wood. It'll just take too long."

"Not if we get a move on." Ruby could be so bossy and unshiftable in this mood and Peter nearly always caved in to her, yet still he pushed on. "When, though?"

"Soon," she snapped. He looked at his watch and sighed, half past eleven, he wished he could just go on instead of having to hang round here, but it wouldn't feel right. He went over to one of the windows, pushed up the sash and looked out; from here you could see down across the cherry orchard where it dipped towards the farm yard and the oast and then – where the land rose up again – there was the Bower Hop Garden and the wood itself, a big sprawl of dark green, so dense and thick there could be a palace and a sleeping princess in the middle of it for all anyone might know. Or a Ghost Man named Gabriel. Peter looked at his watch again, only five minutes had passed. It was no good.

"Come on," he said, "let's just go. It's much tidier now."

"Just a minute." Ruby lined her dolls up in a neat row along the top of her bed, it always made the room look neat once the quilt was straightened and they were in place. Her mum would be satisfied.

"Rubes!" He was already at the top of the stairs.

"Coming!"

She pushed open the door and followed him down.

In the wood

Two nights in a row now Gabriel had seen him, glimpsed more than really caught proper sight of it was true, but enough for him to know that the voice he'd heard a few weeks before belonged to a man he thought he'd never see again in this life. Always in the same place too, down towards the gypsy camp, not one of them though, he had been here long enough to recognise all who came and went to that place, besides they were a companionable people amongst themselves, affectionate in their greetings to one another with a familiar ease that stirred up a homesickness in Gabriel, but for a place and time that in all likelihood, no longer existed.

No, the figure he saw was there for him, a watching shadow following him silently so that when he stopped and waited he heard nothing except the usual sounds of his wood, the tap of a woodpecker, the song of a robin, the startled flurry of a pheasant and always except on the hottest of days – and there were a few of those at the moment – the soft stir of the wind in the tree-tops sounding like the far-off washing of waves on some distant shore. The watcher haunted him and once he had been working with the bird following with his eyes, as she hovered over her prey with a delicate beating stillness of her own and he had caught a movement under the trees not of an animal, but of a man; or what passed for one perhaps. It disturbed him that this could happen so easily that he could be observed by someone he had once known so well and not be aware of it; and sometimes at night in his dreams he saw again those final days when the two of them had last been together, except in his dreams they were always laughing, just as they had in boyhood times when they had cycled up into the mountains, finding warm spots in the flower massed summer meadows to fall on their backs and be amazed at the life they were living.

Now here he was again, having wandered without really meaning to, near the camp. He climbed a little way up into a tree where he could sit and watch and not be seen. From here he could see the boy Oby perched on the gate to the compound where the white goat was kept. Gabriel wished he could jump down and walk over to him, that the two of them might talk about the goat and share stories together, that he might ask about Ruby and the boy Peter. Although he knew it was misguided and probably dangerous, he would have liked to see them again. They had brought life into his lonely existence and a certainty that the world was still going on outside, that a future was possible and time could move along because they were there to make it happen.

So, it was strangely shocking to see them arrive by the gate where Oby sat, to watch them settle on a fallen log and hear their distant laughter. Gabriel almost felt as if he might have conjured them from his own wishfuless. He knew then what he ought to do, he ought to slide quickly from his watching point and disap-pear back to his own part of the wood, but instead he made another choice. Putting his fingers between his lips he whistled, making almost the same sound as he did when he called the bird, similar enough so that the children would know it was him, for it had been something he had shown them that evening, telling them that if ever they needed him to call in this way.

Only now it was him calling to them.

Peter looked at his watch for the third time in about five minutes. "We've got to go, Ruby, or we'll be in trouble." He sounded calm, but he nearly always sounded calm, only Ruby knew that he was getting really agitated.

Oby was sitting a bit further from the three of them, ever since Gabriel had called them into the trees, Oby wasn't sure he wanted to see the man again, or Ruby and Peter. He didn't belong in their life and they didn't belong in his, it was different when they were at school together, then having Ruby as an almost friend felt normal, but in the holidays the difference in the way they lived was sharper and more obvious. And this man, keeping his presence so near to the camp a secret was not something Oby was used to and anyway, most of the others knew about the Ghost Man who walked the woods, why should it matter if he talked about him?

"It takes longer," Peter explained, in case Gabriel was offended. "Ruby can't run so easy with her plaster on."

"You must be careful," Gabriel's voice was slow and sharp-edged, his brown eyes smiled at Ruby. "Thank you for coming, and – " he got up from the ground and brushed himself down, "for telling me."

For the first time Oby spoke, "He is a bad man, Mr. Pierce."

"Yes," echoed Peter, "bad." Although it sounded a bit strong and he knew that for Oby this was true. Stan was one of the people locally always trying to get the camp moved out of the woods, accusing Oby and the rest of being thieving pikies.

"I may not see you again," Gabriel told them.

"No!" Ruby rushed at him and hugged him with her good arm. "And anyway you promised!" Gabriel raised his eyebrows. "You said you'd teach me to fly properly."

"Come on Ruby." Peter was suddenly embarrassed.

"Did I?" While Ruby had lain at the bottom of the tree Gabriel had talked to her and told her many things, he now couldn't remember. He hadn't even been sure that she would have understood what he was saying. It had been such a long time since he had talked to another living person his words once uncorked must have gushed out, perhaps unwisely he realised.

"One day, you said, I would fly properly and see the world from up there!" She flung her hand up in a wild gesture, Peter saw that any minute she might cry. "You promised!"

And Gabriel knelt down beside her, pulled back to a time when his sister, then not much older than Ruby had flung the same accusation, if not the same words, at him for failing to take her swimming in the lake and going off with Herbert and forget-ting all about her. Worse than that, he had said he was going to teach her how to swim and from that day on, with the world going the way it went, there had never been another chance and she never did learn. He wondered if she ever had in all the years that he had been gone, assuming she was still alive. A thought he pushed back into the darkness.

"Yes," said Gabriel, "I shall do my best to make it so for you."

"Are you going to fly back to your home?" Oby surprised everyone.

"Perhaps if it is – " The man's eyes looked up through the trees, but he seemed to be seeing so much more than the patched hot blue sky.

"Ruby." Peter's voice was quiet, something about the Gabriel with them now made him afraid. Not the sort of afraid he got from Stan, this was harder to understand. Peter pulled at Ruby's hand, "Ruby?"

"You could mend it and make it fly again." Oby kicked at the dry earth, pointing the toe of his worn boot and curling the dust into a pattern.

"What?" Gabriel was back with them. "How did you – ?"

And that was how it began, unexpectedly, with Oby surprising them all at what he knew and how he thought about things.

Afterwards, when Gabriel went back to that moment it seemed so obvious that Oby would have followed him without being seen and he wondered, but then dismissed it, if it was Oby's presence he sensed when he knew he was being watched. No, not the boy, who was simply acting with the curiosity of his kind, the watcher was something altogether different and one of the reasons why he must leave.

The Leas

There usually seemed to be so many books, anything she might need, if Ruby looked on the shelves and in the boxes when she went up to the Mission Hut on the Wednesday that was library day, but this week, suddenly she understood that there were gaps. Nothing about planes. Not one. Well, not quite true because there were always loads about that pilot bloke. What she wanted, though, was how to build one. It was a let down. She looked across at where Mrs. Arlott was stacking books, suddenly realising that it was going to look a bit strange, her asking about how to build a plane, it wasn't the kind of thing she'd ever asked for, her usual reading matter was stories, stories, stories. She could never get enough and often just re-read favourites over and over. She'd say it was for Peter, a game they were planning. But would that be too much of a give away? It seemed as if it might be written all over her, the true reason for wanting a book like that. But her mum wanted something as well, she'd written it down, maybe that would help, having the two to ask about.

"This one," Mrs. Arlott reached for a book from a box she had behind the counter, "and this as well, if she likes that one she'd bound to go for this."

"And," Ruby started and it all tumbled out.

"Pardon?" Mrs. Arlott peered at her and smiled. Ruby was one of her best readers and it was because of her that she tried to vary the stock as much as she could, considering the limited supply there was down in the main village branch library.

"Planes," Ruby repeated, "how to make one."

Mrs. Arlott smiled again, "Quite a tall order," she said and wrote something in her notebook. "I'll see what I can rummage," she promised. "For next time."

Two weeks' wait! Patience wasn't one of Ruby's strong points. It seemed such a long time, but there was nothing she could do about it. She picked up her pile, slid them into her big old satchel, hoiked it up on her back. Anyone could tell she didn't want help.

"I'd have given you a hand, if you'd said, dear."

Ruby jumped. Mrs. Pierce, she hadn't noticed her before.

"All right thanks," Ruby mumbled, her cheeks suddenly hot. She hurried out. Mrs. Pierce of all people. It would be. She decided not to tell Peter that bit, stirred up with a sense that he would somehow blame her, although quite for what she wasn't sure.

In the wood

Gabriel woke suddenly. A noise. But what? Not something that he immediately recognised. Not the voice that haunted him more and more during the days when he didn't see the children, as if it was filling the silent space in his head with its old insinuations. No, this was different, a rustling and, as he came to in the dense darkness of his hut, a thin anxious cry, like a child a long way off. He sat up and eased himself slowly off his bed, feeling for the matches and his home-made rush lamp.

"There." He looked towards the opening and caught in the lamp's warm sweep he saw her. His bird, the falcon. Here? And at such an hour, but he soon saw why. One of her wings was bent at an odd, crooked angle, brushing the ground in an awkward movement. She hopped towards him, catching his glance with her own sharp dark eyes and, he thought, if it was possible for a bird to frown then she would be frowning, in obvious pain. He knelt down and shone the light close. It was then that he saw the blood. "How has this happened?" His voice was harsh and pointless in wood's thick silence. He also realised that his question was wrong, not How, but Who? Holding the light closer he saw the place where the shot had entered.

Later, as dawn started to break, Gabriel finished tending her, cleaning the wound and applying some salve, having made, as best he could for the moment, a temporary splint to help keep the wing straight. When daylight came he would take her outside to the clearing and see how she moved.

As he sat with her, trying to calm her and prevent her from trying to move about too much and damage the already injured wing further, he rolled the thoughts in his head. He wanted to believe that the shooting was some kind of mistake, that maybe whoever had done it was aiming for a pigeon or other game bird and she happened to be in the line of fire. Yet, even as he turned these thoughts over again, he knew that this had the mark of a deliberate act. He unclenched his fist; the evidence was here, in the palm of his hand, the bullet he had removed from the point where her wing joined her breast. He shuddered at the cruelty of it and at the bird's vulnerability and then wondered at himself, getting so worked up about a wild thing that by its nature was constantly dishing out and risking death. This was such a small event in the huge wash of what had so recently happened in the world and in which he'd willingly played a part, compounding it with one final cut that had left him here adrift and far from all he had known and loved as a boy.

"Come, come now," he murmured to her, stroking the top of her head and marvelling at the softness and how vividly it contrasted with the scimitar-sharp curve of her beak and the cold blinking of her dark eyes. She was shifting herself and casting quick looks at the open doorway. He knew he would have to tether her, which she would not like, but if he was to find food for both of them, he had to be able to leave her and un-tethered she would surely want to escape the dark confines of his hut. He gave her some more water and then remembered that he still had the remains of a rabbit stew, enough to satisfy her until he could go hunting. He would, he thought, make some traps and catch the kind of small rodent that should please her and give her a sense of safety and trust. Although, he knew she did indeed trust him, their two years together had proved that.

Coming back to his hut an hour or so later he stopped and ducked behind the young oak that formed the ring of trees edging this almost-clearing. He could see that there was movement inside and more movement than the bird could make. He held his breath and again, the picture of Herbert came to him with such detail it might have been days rather than years since they had last met. Those winter blue eyes with their corner creases of laughter lines, his corn-stubble head, or so Gabriel had teased him, in their youth Herbert had favoured longer hair, a flop of curls constantly being shaken back of his forehead.

"Herbert?" He whispered, listening. "Herbert?" Louder this time, but even as the name hushed into the still blue of the morning air, Gabriel didn't really believe it could be true.

"Mr. Gabriel?" A small figure stepped from the square dark of the doorway and into the light.

She seemed to have come, unusually, alone this time. Peter, she explained, when he asked, was following on later. What she didn't tell him was that they'd had a row. Having got to Oby's and found, once again, that he was away down with his uncle and aunt at the site by the river, Peter had said they should go home, that he wanted to get back and work on the drawings he'd started on how planes were built, but she'd wanted to come and see Gabriel, talk to him, not be stuck indoors when the weather was so good and any other time she'd be looking for a good tree to climb. And so, here she was.

"What happened to your falcon?" Ruby squinted up at him. They were sitting outside, sipping hot sweet tea from tin cups. She had hers propped on her plaster.

"She was shot. Someone shot her." He couldn't keep the anger from his voice and Ruby flinched momentarily.

"Why?"

"I don't know why," he said and then smiled, tapping at her plaster. "But you are two of a kind, eh?"

Ruby looked at the bird, Gabriel had moved her outside, so that she too could feel the sun on her. "Same side, as well," Ruby said, "my left arm and her left wing. Is it broken too?"

"Well, I think it maybe not broken. I hope, anyway. Grazed by the bullet, so very sore for her and difficult to fly at the moment."

"You talk funny," Ruby observed, half to herself, sipping more of the tea.

"I'm sorry," Gabriel said, amused at his need to apologise to this child.

"S'all right," she said. "If we get better at the same time, we could fly off up, up into the sky together." She stared up through the tree canopy, up there already in her mind's eye, Gabriel realised.

"That is a nice thought." He wouldn't lie to her, not if he could help it.

"You mean I can't, not fly like she does, anyway?"

"There are other ways."

"In planes," Ruby nodded. "But it's not the same."

"No," Gabriel said, "I don't suppose it is."

"You said I could fly, though. That time, when we were waiting for Peter, when I hurt myself, broke my arm. You said that one day you'd help, but you were just saying that weren't you?" She glared at him.

"I know that it is something you really want to do, Ruby, and if I can I shall help you, but it is a complicated thing what you ask. Flying in a plane is so much easier, but you are quite correct to say that it is a different thing. It is." He stared into his cup, swilling the dregs round as if they might give him the answer.

"Tell me." She sat, hand propped under her chin, staring up at him with her saucer eyes.

"Tell you what?" He asked, smiling.

"What it's like," she jerked her head towards the sky, "when you're flying."

Gabriel closed his eyes for a moment, and suddenly there it was, the hot, sharp picture of his first night flight. Lights telling of many lives scattered below in the darkness, like stars mirrored in dark waters. All those people he would never meet, never know, whose existence was as a dream might be, men, women, children, sleeping in the safe warmth of their beds, or staring into the dying fire in the hearth, reading a book by lamplight, listening to a lullaby or a story.

A picture much like a child's drawing, patterned with small, faraway details, mapped out far below and then quickly lost as the plane flew into clouds and then out again, upwards, where real stars netted the blackness with their own swarming glitter of light.

Then a later picture of bright flares booming out in the dark landscape beneath, snatching out those earlier fires of life.

But he didn't tell Ruby about that part of the story.

When he stopped, she was staring at him even more intently, frowning, trying to see it all for herself, he guessed, wanting to be up there too, hungry for the reality of it.

"So," she whispered half to herself, "like when I climb the oak tree on top of the Mound."

"Yes," he said. "I expect it is."

"And one day you'll show me," she said, still caught in the dreaminess of it all.

"I shall try my best," he said, after a moment. "That much I can promise."

Then Ruby banged her cup against her head and laughed, believing him and coming out of the dream, remembering why it had been so important that she come and see him today.

"I'm getting a book for you," she said.

His reading matter had consisted mostly of books left behind by hop-pickers, romances mostly, and old newspapers, some of these he'd kept to remind himself of why he was here, but he was touched by Ruby's declaration. "Stories, huh? I have always liked stories, that is very kind of you."

"No, no," she frowned at him, "not stories, but I can bring you some of those if you like. It's going to be about building an aeroplane. Mrs. Arlott promised she'd find it for me."

"Mrs. Arlott?" Gabriel felt a rush of fear. Was this yet another person who knew about him?

"At the Library on the Leas," Ruby explained, "I asked if she could get me a book on planes."

"And what else did you tell her?" He tried to keep his voice even.

Ruby thought for a moment, not sure what he meant. "My mum wanted a book too."

"You have not spoken about me?" Gabriel found it difficult to ask this question and another rang inside his head, what was he going to do if she had?

"We crossed our hearts and all." Ruby was offended. "'Course we shan't tell."

"Yes, yes, you are right." He took a breath. "Thank you, Ruby, for thinking about the book."

"That's all right," she said, "I'll bring some of mine too, if you like."

"And," he frowned, "can I ask you one thing other?"

She nodded and smiled at him.

"To bring to me some newspapers? Yes? This would be good."

"Yes," she said and skipped off humming, his questions made her happy.

Peter was never one to hold a grudge, or keep a row going beyond its natural time and a moment later there he was, mooching from out of the trees, whistling quietly in that way he had, hoping that a bird would answer. They often did and it was often a robin. Now, though, it was Gabriel's bird, responding with a slow peep, as if Peter might be another of her kind, come to set her free.

The farm

Ruby was standing on the old kitchen chair just outside the back door. From here she could see the distant soft smear of green that was the edge of Bower Wood. It had been a week now since they'd seen Gabriel. Only another few days and she could get the book for him, if Mrs. Arlott had managed to find one. Ruby wondered if the bird's wing was better. She could hardly feel the twinges from her arms now, just the itching from the plaster, that was almost unbearable in the never-ending heat of the summer. Down in the cherry orchard the geese were kicking up their usual fuss at the water trough. Bloody lot of squabblers, her dad called this year's goslings.

"You listening, Ruby?" Her mum was reaching up holding the jam jar.

"Sorry."

"Careful, now." She hadn't wanted Ruby to climb up there in the first place, but the jar needed replacing and Ruby had been desperate to get up there, her mum could see that. The long hot spell had produced a plague of wasps and catching them in an unwashed jam jar, three quarters full of water at least helped to keep the numbers down in the house.

Once down Ruby dodged inside and checked the clock. "Blimey! Supposed to be at the Mound in five minutes." It was a good ten minutes' walk away too, and then there was the picnic to carry. It had been tricky enough to arrange with Oby in the first place; if they were late he might just go and think they'd changed their minds. She wondered where Peter had got to, he was bringing the squash.

The Mound

In the end Peter went racing off on his bike just to make sure. By the time Ruby got there they were already knocking back the orange squash and acting as if they'd been friends forever, when really it was Ruby who'd started it all. Not only that, but they'd got the best spot under the tree too, right in the middle, where she always sat. Good climbing tree this one, too, if you didn't have your arm in plaster.

"Budge up." She flopped down next to Peter.

He passed her the bottle and she gulped back the warm squash, wishing she'd brought another bottle.

"Oby says he's seen Gabriel."

"Oh?" Now here was another sore spot. Mr. Gabriel was hers, surely? Now even he seemed to be getting away from her.

Oby rolled over and held out a handful of cherries. She took some, made ear-rings from two pairs and started eating the rest, spitting stones into the long goose grass.

"When d'you see him?" She'd pushed her way in between them and managed to get into the best spot, after all.

"Last night, he came to the edge of our camp. He wanted to know if I had seen his falcon."

"But she'd hurt her wing; someone had shot her – he said." She glared at him as if it might have been him, although she knew it hadn't. Oby loved animals, he even thanked the rabbits, he'd told her, the ones they caught for their stews. She'd liked the idea of that and had secretly started doing it at home under her breath at meal times.

"Had you, then?" Ruby asked.

"No, and I told him No, but later on he came back."

"It's a sad ending, Ruby," Peter warned, wondering if his handkerchief was clean enough to give her.

Oby hesitated and looked over at Peter who nodded and carried on with the story. "He found her near the goat pen."

"Was she all right?" But she knew the answer.

"Dead," Oby put in quickly, as if it could be less of a thing. He made a throat cutting gesture before Peter could stop him.

"Why? But I don't get it!" She looked first at Peter and then Oby, as if they might be deliberately keeping it from her.

Oby was stirring at the dusty ground with his finger and shaking his head as if the whole business was too big a puzzle to comment on.

"I don't get it." Ruby said again. "She was going to get better, he said, Mr. Gabriel – "

"Gabriel, just Gabriel, Ruby!" Peter snapped.

"He said she would get better." She couldn't find her breath to say more. It all seemed wrong.

"You don't understand." Oby stared hard at her. "Someone had found her and cut her throat. It wasn't the shooting that killed her. And the worst part – " Now another shock. Oby was crying and for a moment Peter wasn't sure who needed his handkerchief first.

"Here," Peter said, choosing Oby. He wasn't much of a crier

himself and it was strange seeing Oby, usually so withheld, in this state. It must be bad, whatever it was.

"Oby?" Ruby leaned across and touched the back of his hand.

"He thinks it was me," Oby said, looking from one to the other, shaking his head, still not believing that anyone would think he'd harm a creature in this way, surely everyone knew that.

"No." Ruby looked at him.

"He does, he thinks I did it." Oby ran through it again in his mind. How he'd gone to check on the goats and found the kestrel, cold to touch, blood already drying across the soft tawny feathers of her throat. Just as he picked her up, Gabriel had appeared silently behind him. His anger almost knocked Oby over and the string of words hit him like stones in his gut. Upset by what he'd found Oby couldn't take in or understand, yes, that was it, he simply couldn't understand what Gabriel was barking at him. But it made him want to shrink into something too small to be noticed by something as ferocious as this. Before he'd had a chance to answer Gabriel had snatched the bird from him and disappeared back into the trees.

"Didn't you tell him?" Peter was sure it could be cleared up, Gabriel wouldn't put the blame on Oby like this.

"He wouldn't listen," He rubbed his eyes and handed the handkerchief back to Peter. Now he'd told the story he felt better, these two, his friends, hadn't even had to say that it was wrong, it was written between them strong and unspoken.

"We must go and see him," Ruby was already on her feet. "Come on."

Peter and Oby stared at her, the last thing Oby wanted to do was to face that anger again; he shook his head and fixed his eyes on the thin lip of sea on the far horizon, wishing he could be there and out of all this muddle.

Gradually, the familiar comfort of the place calmed them, they ate their sandwiches, drank the squash and sat for a while playing I-Spy, with Ruby nearly always choosing something to do with birds, flying or trees. Both the boys teased her until she threatened to bash them with her plaster. Soon the afternoon passed into the gentler warmth of early evening and it was time for Oby to go back. Their shadows bobbed and stretched together, then separated as they walked down the track that led from the Mound to the farm, Ruby hung behind and signalled to Peter to wait. "Is there time?"

"What for?"

"Tonight, you know." She whispered hard at him, finally getting the satisfaction of knocking him with her plastered arm.

"Not sure."

"We have to," Ruby said. She hated anyone to think badly of Oby, it was the same at school, Peter sometimes wondered if she'd stick up for him in the same way, but mostly it didn't bother him.

"Don't see how. What are we going to say?"

Ruby stopped and crouched down to examine a stone that was lodged in the side of the bank, she was always on the look-out for more Shepherds' Crowns, fossils of starfish from the long ago time when the sea was more than a distant gleam from the top of the Mound.

"Say to who?" Oby, who'd been slow to leave their spot on the Mound had finally caught up with them.

"No one," Ruby said, too quickly, so that as they started walking again, Oby dropped behind once more.

"Peter?" Ruby nudged him again.

"All right," Peter whispered, "I'll have a think." If he could please her, he would. That was how it always was.

In the wood

He buried her where the trees thinned out by the side of the wide flat meadow that had been one of her favourite hunting spots, right in the middle of a great scatter of moon daisies.

Sitting back on his haunches afterwards, he considered again whether it had been the boy Oby, a snag of doubt troubled him. It would be an easy explanation; a gypsy killing what was needed for the pot, no matter how graceful the creature. Hadn't he done the same when hunger knocked?

And yet.

If not the boy then who? For it would seem to be an act of wanton brutality, with no purpose other than to destroy. He caught the whisper then, that familiar voice: "It's how they are, all rotten within, damaging the good healthy stock that supports them! Pruning is a necessary evil, eh Gabriel? Otherwise they will bring us down with them in the end."

Walking back through the wood he heard the sound of something, or someone approaching. Someone? The thought brushed him that this might be the killer of his bird come to gloat or do more harm, perhaps to him this time. He felt for the blade in his pocket, cool and smooth. Ready if needed. He recalled his days of training in the woods of home in that other time and stopped behind a beech tree, still young but thick enough in trunk to provide some cover. Whoever, or whatever was coming his way also stopped. Waiting.

"Herbert?" Did he speak or just think the name, he couldn't tell.

There was a faint movement which might have been the first stir of the evening breeze. He whistled, but softly, much as he used to when calling her and the act of making this sound brought a lump to his throat.

"He's whistling," a voice said. "That's him," said another. So, they had come and late in the day too. He stepped out and went towards them.

Back at his hut he made tea for them all with some that they had brought, there were more supplies too, including some tobacco that Ruby had found in a tin in the shed, kept there and half forgotten by her dad for when he was working in there on rainy days. They had wanted to see the grave first and Ruby had picked a bunch of foxgloves and purple cranesbill to sit among the daisies on the small mound. "Rest in Peace," she'd said and bowed her head, a few tears slipping down her face. Peter patted her back and said nothing, but knew she was most likely thinking about Blackness. It didn't seem right to talk about who'd done it, there by the grave, so they had walked in silence to Gabriel's hut, almost, but not quite, unseen in the dusk dimming light under the trees.

"We came to say it wasn't Oby," Peter announced quietly in Ruby's ear, worried that their reason might get forgotten, the way Ruby chatted on and on to Gabriel, telling him about the books and how they'd help and how long did he think it was likely to take and about their picnic that afternoon on the Mound and how next time he must come.

"Oby," repeated Peter.

"It wasn't Oby," Ruby said. "He didn't kill her, that's why we've come. To tell you." She put her good hand out and lightly touched Gabriel's arm to show it was true. "He found her just before you came, he said she was lying there like she'd been put there on purpose."

"Well, yes, that much I had guessed." Gabriel wasn't usually so sharp with Ruby, Peter thought he was most likely still upset. It was a sad thing to think they would never again watch Gabriel's bird come to him when he whistled and settle on his arm and swivel her head to stare at him, but only him, with her deep wild-dark eyes. Then he would stretch out his arm, lift it and off she'd fly, once back to him and then high up or off into the distance on her own business where none of them could follow or know.

"He loves animals," Ruby went on unshaken. "He would never do anything to hurt a bird as beautiful as her." She thought for a moment. "Did she have a name?"

"Yes," said Gabriel. He closed his eyes. "Little One."

"Pretty," sighed Ruby who thought it sounded like an Indian princess. "Little One," she repeated.

"You do believe us?" Peter was worried because Gabriel hadn't said Oh, that's all right then, or No, I didn't think it really was Oby, which is what they wanted to hear.

Gabriel opened his eyes and looked first up through the gap in the tree canopy at the gold stained glow of sky and then at each of them. His face was serious. "Yes," he answered, "I believe that Oby did not kill her. The question is, who did?" And deep in his head the voice was saying Should you really be talking to these children in this way? Perhaps you have spent too long away from the company of men.

"We'll find out for you," Ruby's eyes shone with the excitement of it, in stories it was always the children who uncovered this kind of crime. They'd do it, with Oby's help too.

"I am very lucky to have met you, yes?" Gabriel stood up, smiling at last, emptying the dregs of his tea before taking their mugs. It was time for them to go. Peter was relieved, the way Ruby was she looked as if she'd stay there forever.

"Please," added Gabriel, "do not get into trouble. No?"

"No," promised Ruby, turning round to wave as she followed Peter into the now dark wood, "and we'll come back next week, when the books come and I'll bring the papers."

"You are taking such a risk, my friend." The voice caught Gabriel as he ducked inside his hut. Looking back into the now empty clearing and the trees beyond he could see no one. He stood and listened, waiting. No, nothing. Perhaps tonight he would sleep without the dreams, steadied as he was by the clear innocent sureness of the two children. He pulled his rough made door closed behind him though and put the bar across, just to be on the safe side.

Out beyond his little hidden clearing somewhere near the wood's edge, maybe, a nightingale started to sing, and a shadow moved steady and fast soon lost in the wash of the dark.

The oast house

The smell was always the same, dust, oil, sacking and hops, mixed and mashed together forever into the walls of the building. Sunlight clear and bright outside, struggled in through the windows, the squared panes coated and filmed by the dust of years, a century most likely, since the oast was built in 1857, according to the engraving on the wall. So long ago, it might have always been there.

"Come on, Ruby," Mum scolded, but gently, "you hold this end." She put the end of the blanket into her hand. It was Monday morning and they were helping to sort out the building ready for the men to move in during hop picking. Ruby and her mum were in the bunk room, where the men slept and ate during the picking season, keeping an eye on the driers, making sure nothing caught fire and everything was safe.

Ruby jumped as there was a sudden shuffling sound from underneath one of the bottom bunks. "Minnie the Mooch!" She dropped the blanket and bent down to try and pick up the cat who wouldn't be held, but leapt onto the table, where she sat washing her mottled amber fur and pulling at her claws as if it what was she'd planned to do all along. "Minnie," Ruby cooed and stroked her carefully. The farm cats chose their company and seldom liked being overly petted.

"It's queer without Blackness, eh?" Her mum stood next to her and put her hand on Ruby's shoulder.

"Yes," Ruby found it hard to think about Blackness without wanting to cry and although Dad had said they should maybe get another cat – one of Minnie's daughter's kittens perhaps – it still didn't feel right. Not yet. And Mum reckoned that a cat always found you if it wanted a home, so maybe there was one out there, somewhere, still looking. Meantime, there were always cats around on the farm, fed by the housekeeper at the farmhouse and living comfortably in the barn where the shoddy sacks were stored. Must be like sleeping on cushions, Ruby thought, all those rags from people's clothes stuffed into sacks, used for manuring the hop gardens. And Minnie was queen of them all, everyone knew that.

"You are so pretty," Ruby whispered into Minnie's ear, tickling it and wondering at the silky touch of a thing as ordinary as an ear. Her own never felt as soft. Minnie purred rough and steady, sounding like the engine of a far-off tractor. It was a rare treat her staying for so long to be petted like this. Ruby's mum let them be and carried on folding the blankets, one for each of the four bunks, aired and ready for making up nearer the time.

Only the cat heard the footsteps outside the door and was soon down and ready to make a dash, hesitating for a moment when she saw who it was, unsure of the best escape route. It was clear she didn't like having to pass so close to this man's feet.

"Mr. Pierce," Mum said, "there you are." She took the pile of flannel sheets from him and started sorting them.

"Stan," he told her, glancing down as Minnie greased past him.

"I beg your pardon?" Mum could sound so distant sometimes.

"Stan," he repeated, fixing her with a cold stare from his dirty grey eyes. Ruby shivered, it often happened near him. She was glad she wasn't here on her own.

"Well," Mum was not one to be bossed about, "thank you for the sheets, in any case."

"How's that arm of yours?" He spat back into the dusty gloom and Ruby tried to memorize where it landed, so she wouldn't accidentally walk on the place.

"Getting better," Mum answered before she could speak. "Plaster'll be off next week maybe, eh Ruby?" She ruffled Ruby's head as if to say it was all on account of her being so clever, surely, that the plaster could come off sooner than everyone had thought.

"Best stay away from them woods, then, eh?" He laughed as if it was a joke they all shared, but really it sounded more like the way the boys in the playground laughed when one of them managed to trip someone up ever so accidentally on purpose.

"Well, it'll still take a while to heal," Mum said, "so she'll not be falling out of any more trees for the moment." She turned round to face the window, which meant that her back was now towards Stan, but still he didn't take the hint.

"Not just trees you have to watch out for though, is it?" His stare was on Ruby, making her want to run away just like the cat had done, if only she could scoot past and on out into the clean sunlight.

"Wells," Ruby blurted, wanting to push him off the scent. He raised his eyebrows, his face still smeared with that pretend grin he carried.

"Wells?" Mum turned to look at her.

"Yes, you know Mum, all the wells in Bower Wood, we have to be ever so careful, but me and Peter know where lots of them are and so does Oby, so it's all right. Really."

"Wells, eh?" Stan echoed and then he spat again, looked from one to the other shaking his head as if they might have gone mad and he was the sane one amongst the crazy people, and he turned and strolled off, whistling.

"Funny, that." Mum was shaking her head and Ruby was afraid she was going to be rumbled over all that smoke screen of well jabber.

"What's funny?"

"Man like him, whistling like that, easy as pie and such a pretty tune too."

Later, when they were back home sitting in the garden under the apple tree having a cup of tea, at least Mum was, while Ruby sat and twiddled round the ropes of the swing so that she could whiz round fast when they untwisted, Stan's name came up again, in a roundabout way.

"Mum?"

"Mm?" She had her eyes closed, but she wasn't asleep.

"Do you like everybody?" Ruby and Peter were always arguing about this, because mostly Peter did seem to like everybody, at least he didn't ever seem to dislike people; he just didn't have much to do with the ones he couldn't get on with, that's what he told Ruby when she pushed him. She, on the other hand, found there were several people she didn't like, Susan Scribbs, one of the girls in the top class who thought she was special because she lived in house in the castle grounds, but really it was because her dad was a gardener, Head Gardener she said.

"Do I like everybody?" Mum opened her eyes and reached for her cup of tea left cooling on the old low wall.

"Yes." Ruby let the rope unwind and the hot afternoon light whirled past her in a mash of blue and green.

"No. Why?"

"Just wondered." She frowned as another thought came into her head. "How do you know? Whether you like someone or not?"

"Sometimes you just do, you meet a person and you know you're not going to take to them, or the other way round too. You meet someone and you just click."

"Like Peter and me?" Ruby remembered how they'd sat next to one another in Infants' and then Peter's dad had started on the farm as Stockman soon afterwards, but by this time they were already friends, there were people who didn't know who sometimes thought they were brother and sister.

"Yes, I'd say you two clicked." Her mum smiled, thinking back to those days too, how they'd been worried that Ruby might be lonely out here with no brothers or sisters, and even all the cousins lived in another part of the county. Peter had changed that and Oby too, perhaps.

"And Oby too?" she said aloud.

"Yes."

But Ruby thought that it had been different with Oby and maybe always would be, he was a friend, but not like Peter, separate, a friend yet on the outside, the edge, like the other creatures that lived in the wood. And, then, there was Gabriel, but he mustn't be talked of. She sighed and dragged the toe of one of her sandals in the worn dusty patch under the swing as she pushed herself slowly to and fro.

"He's a nice boy, Oby." Her mum gave her a sideways look. "It's all right, is it?"

"What?"

"Between the three of you?"

"Well, Peter sometimes gets cross with me." Ruby realised that's what had changed, when the three of them were together, he would snap if she got things wrong, like Gabriel not being Mister and all that. As if she was being daft and he'd suddenly just noticed.

"He's a good friend," her mum said, "and I'll surmise he always will be."

"Mmm," Ruby was only half-listening. "Mr. Pierce – " she stopped, not sure what she was trying to say.

"What about him?"

"I don't like him," Ruby said.

"No," her mum agreed, "neither do I."

And perhaps it was then, or maybe it had been earlier in the oast that morning, but it unblocked a thought in Ruby's head about Gabriel's bird. She needed to go and find Peter.

The camp

Usually it would be difficult to creep up on Oby in these woods, he knew the meaning of most sounds. Yet here it was happening for the second time in a matter of days and the same person too, choosing a moment when no one else was near. He felt the soft touch of a hand on his back and whirled round ready to run.

"I have come to say that I am sorry for being angry for thinking that you – " The man shrugged and shook his head. He felt foolish and tainted again by the wrong he had done to another.

"I understand," Oby told him, but his eyes moved to take in the shadows among the trees behind Gabriel. "It was a cruel thing. Maybe you'll find another kestrel?"

Gabriel stared at him, made nervous by the boy's wary shifting glance. "Another?" Then understanding came. "Oh, perhaps, but – " He shrugged again. "There may not be time. It took two years for her to trust me in that way, you know."

"Yes," said Oby, who did. "I'm sorry it happened. Ruby and Peter – "

"The two – " and Gabriel used a word Oby had never heard, he knew it was meant in a friendly way, though, and so he nodded and went on: "They think they might find out who did it."

Gabriel smiled a sad smile at the ground and huffed. "Perhaps," he murmured, "it is possible. But I do not want them to get into trouble because of it. You will tell them. Yes?"

"All right," Oby nodded, wondering why the man was so concerned. Couldn't he tell them himself the next time he saw them? Another movement caught his eye back along the path where Gabriel had appeared. "You have been followed?" Surely this man who could surprise him so easily, would sense someone on his track?

Gabriel looked back towards the trees and muttered more words that Oby couldn't quite catch, then he caught the boy's hand in his again. "I am sorry," he repeated, "for all of it." Then before Oby could ask him what he meant by that he had slid off in another direction, soon lost among the denser darkness of the tree canopy, made heavier, somehow, by the dazzle of bright sun that flowed into the clearing where Oby now stood alone.

The farm

There was a haystack down by the bottom edge of the cherry orchard, in a space between where the orchard ended and the top end of Saxon hop garden began. Just behind and to the left ran the wall to the pig sties, and further along was the tar pit, so the smells were always a rich mix at certain times of year of fruit, hops, hay, pigs and tar. When there wasn't really time to go to the Mound it was where Peter and Ruby would meet to talk over secret business. Years later it would be the pungent oily-sharp tar smell that would take Ruby back to that place and the hushed companionship she and Peter shared during that summer.

"There's no proof," Peter said after Ruby had finished. He passed her the lemonade bottle. "Want some?"

She took it and drank, feeling the warm sticky spill run down her neck as she lay stretched on the hay, eyes half closed against the dazzle of blue sky.

"We'd have to find evidence," he said, tickling his arm with a loose strand of hay. It made him feel drowsy.

"I just know," Ruby said. "He's not – " There was a word that fitted, but she couldn't think of it. "I don't like him."

Peter humphed, eyes closed.

"And nor does Mum."

"I don't like him neither," Peter said, "but it doesn't mean he killed the bird."

"Supposing, though, if he did then it means he knows about Gabriel and everything."

"Everything?" Peter snorted, annoyed with himself for not having thought of that.

Ruby sat up, "We should go and tell him, in case."

"All right," he said, not moving.

"When?" Ruby could never wait for anything. He knew she meant now.

"I'm not sure."

"We should." But she knew she couldn't go on her own.

Peter rolled on to his side and squinted at her. "He might get worried if we do. He might go away sooner before we've had a chance to help him and everything."

Ruby hadn't thought of that and there was his promise too, that he'd help her to fly like she wanted and this Wednesday there might be a book on how to build planes. It would be risky, telling him, and just for the sake of horrible Stan. Her dad didn't like him either, although he'd never said, she could tell, he didn't work with him unless he had to.

"It most likely was him, though," Peter said now, having turned it over properly in his head. It was just the kind of nasty thing Stan would do, he never seemed to like to see anyone having a good time without trying to spoil it. Peter's mum reckoned it was to do with having been in the army during the war; she said it had changed a lot of people, her own dad for one who'd never been the same after he was demobbed. He didn't really know what she meant, but it seemed to make her sad and she'd tell him to get out from under her feet and couldn't he go out and play.

"Most likely was," echoed Ruby, "and one day he'll get found out, just you wait and see."

And that was it, a warm summer's day, snatches of soft white cloud making the deep blue sky seem like the sea sprinkled with islands, bees drowsing in the hedges heavy with pollen and that familiar smell, hay, pigs, tar and the two of them hatching their plans.

In the wood

When Oby had told what he already knew and what he had known for many weeks now, Gabriel realised he must be more careful. He also began to wonder if he should just head for the sea and find his way home in a more ordinary fashion than the one he had concocted. How easy would it be? He turned these thoughts over and over in his mind, alone in his wanderings, with now not even the steadying company of the bird to soften the hard edged loneliness that was beginning to eat into him, darkening his thoughts about himself, the past and all the wrongs he and his kind had brought to the world. The children had made him see that even more clearly; weren't they the innocents that spoke for all those others? It was a pain that ate at him and made him question going home, afraid of what he might discover there, not just those he loved who might not have survived, but those he loved who had.

That night after seeing the gypsy boy he decided not to sleep in his hut as usual, but to rig up the hammock he had occasionally used over the years on hot summer nights. It meant he was high up in the branches of a beech tree, cradled like a child, out of sight from anything or anyone below. Yet, he told himself, it was the kind of thing he and Herbert used to do in the forests of home, so he would know where to look, if he was to come that night. Gabriel laughed at his foolishness then. What use would any hiding place be against Herbert's seeking? Nevertheless, he climbed up and settled into his sailor's bed and lay for a long time catching glimpses of stars pricking through the top canopy and Jupiter sailing up into view, diamond bright, and listening to the sounds of the wood at night, the thin shuffle of leaves as the tree itself seemed to settle into rest.

Eventually, he slept.

Later, down through the wood on the edge of the camp, a figure moved slow and silent. Carrying his knife again, he unlatched the gate to the goat's pen and slid inside.

The Leas

Peter had come this time and not just because Ruby had asked him to. He went through moods with books, sometimes reading anything he could lay his hands on, even the newspaper, but especially comics, and stories about the Romans; he was mad on those, real and made-up. It was always him suggesting digging up bits of Roman Fields and wanting to explore the caves under the Mound, because there was bound to be something worth finding. He'd already got a biscuit tin full of china fragments that were most likely not that old, except for one that was red and patterned with what could have been a bull, but neither of them was sure about it and Peter said they should take into the museum next time they were in town, which wasn't very often. Or when they did go no one quite remembered.

Today, though, Ruby was happy that he'd come with her, he

could help carry stuff for one thing, it was tiring only being able to use one arm, and more than that, she felt safer when he was around and he could back her up with the story about their game and everything.

Mrs. Arlott had managed to find the book they needed, too; admittedly it was how to build toy planes, but surely the big ones couldn't be that different? And Gabriel knew all about them, so it wouldn't be too hard to work it all out. Ruby was happy and there was another travelling theatre story she hadn't read before and the books for Mum. No sign of Mrs. Pierce in the library today either. On the way out Ruby stopped and pushed open the lid of the piano in the hall that was used for parties and village whist drives. Peter was already standing in the porch, staring up towards the shop, they'd promised themselves ice lollies to eat on the walk back through the fields. It was another hot day in the long trail of hot days that made this summer and his throat was dry.

"Just coming." Ruby heard his sigh, but she wanted to trail her fingers across the keys, she'd always wanted a piano of her own and this was the nearest she'd got. Sometimes, when she went to Sunday School here, Mrs. Arlott (who ran that too) would let her try and pick out hymns for them all to sing along to. Once the plaster was off, Ruby decided, she'd come up and practise some more and maybe one day she'd learn to read music.

"What d'you think?" They were sitting on some empty fruit boxes in Roman Field finishing the lollies, unspokenly seeing who could make theirs last longer. Peter had been studying the book on planes.

"It's going to be hard," he said, "we'll need a lot of wood."

"Well?" Wasn't there loads of it lying all over Bower Wood, bits left and half-forgotten by the bodgers who worked there making chairs and other sorts of furniture?

"A lot of wood," Peter repeated, noticing Ruby's licked-clean lolly stick. He'd won again, it was too easy sometimes.

Ruby shrugged. "Gabriel'll know what to do and any case, won't there be some left from the plane, you know?"

It was strange, they'd hardly talked about the hidden plane and yet without it none of this would be happening and, Ruby thought suddenly, Gabriel would maybe stay in the wood forever and be there for them to visit and think about. Their secret, bigger than anything they'd had before. It had been a bit like finding that fairies really did exist after all, only this was a different kind of magic. And, come to think of it, they hadn't actually seen the plane, not yet, only Oby. It was a queer thought.

"Oby!" She stood up.

"What about him?" Peter squinted at her.

She turned and screwed up her face, as if he'd just said something mad and weird, when really it was her own thought that made her frown. "Don't know." She stared off to another place, it happened now and then and Peter was used to it.

"Come on," he said, tugging at her good arm, "we should go."

"All right," she said and followed, but still not quite there, still frowning while small tears of sweat gathered into the creases of her forehead.

It was as they reached the end of the track that led out on to the farm lane, that Ruby spoke again. "I've got this feeling," she said.

"Yes?" Peter had climbed up to sit on the top of the gate, permanently propped open here and a good spot for sitting under the shade of a may tree, where small berries were already forming for summer's end. He waited, it was one of the things he did best and lately had forgotten about – a little.

"Just a feeling." She slumped against his legs.

"Ouch!"

"Sorry."

"What about?" He shifted so she could lean more comfortably for both of them.

"It's hard." Ruby squirled at the sun-dried grass with the toe of her sandal. "Like I heard him calling me, or something. Like he's in trouble. See?"

"Yes," Peter said, who didn't really. Not yet.

"You think I'm going do-lally."

"No." She'd said this kind of thing before, he remembered, but not for a long while now.

"What do you want to do, then?" He pulled at a long strand of grass and began stroking it up and down his arm.

Ruby didn't answer, but it was obvious. They'd have to go and check. He slid down off the gate and picked up the pile of books. "Let's take these home and then go up to the camp then, eh?"

The farm

It was strange seeing Oby sitting on their back steps, blinking up at them as they came round the corner with their clutch of books. For a minute no one spoke and then words fell out in a tangle.

"Oby – ?"

"Sorry," Oby said and got up.

"What's up?" Peter spoke for the first time and Ruby kicked at a loose brick. She'd wanted to ask first.

"My goat," Oby explained.

"Your special one?" Ruby said.

"Yes, Nancy. Nancy," he said again, softly, as if to someone else.

"She's dead isn't she?"

"Ruby!" Peter gave her a hard stare, shocked himself now.

"Yes," Oby whispered, suddenly covering his face with his hands. Was he crying again? He never cried, not even when people called him names, threw stones even. He never cried. Ruby sank down next to him, putting her good arm round his shoulders.

"Her throat, blood," his voice muffled through his hands.

"What d'you mean?" Ruby thought he must mean some kind of accident. Had Nancy got out of the pen? Been run over by someone? No, that was daft, surely, how many cars drove down that track? And if they did, not very fast, it was too narrow, too bumpy.

"Killed?" Peter asked.

"Yes." Oby wrenched his hands from his face and smeared away the traces of tears. Peter pulled out one of his big handkerchiefs and handed it to him.

"Killed?" Ruby wondered if she'd heard right. Then it dawned and she thought about Gabriel's bird. Someone was going round killing things, just out of spite and she knew who.

After Oby had told his story they all sat still and quiet for a while. It was so horrible, the picture of Nancy lying there in the pen, bleeding to death. Oby coming every morning as he always did to bring her some special treat. She was his favourite, he'd nursed her with a baby's bottle when she was a kid, after her mother had died in the birthing.

"What about the others?" Peter asked.

"They were in another pen that night. Nancy had a sore place on her foot and my aunty was coming today to bring some of her special ointment and she said to keep her separate, case it was catching." He looked at Ruby, seeing her properly now.

"Aunty Mina?" Ruby said, nodding.

"Yes." Oby nodded too.

Ruby wasn't sure how to say what she had in her head without upsetting him again. She nudged Peter.

"What?" His breath was warm in her ear.

"Let's go in for a minute, get some lemonade?"

"Why?" he whispered back.

"Goat."

"Huh?"

"Stan," Ruby nudged him harder this time. She patted Oby on the shoulder, like her mum did to her when she was upset. "Just going in to get us a drink. Back in a minute. All right?"

Oby shook his head, looking up at her, but not seeing her.

Standing by the sink in the cool darkness of the kitchen Ruby felt even more sure. "It was Stan," she said, "killed the bird and now Oby's goat. Bet you."

"Well – it could be." Peter was always slow to jump.

"It is!"

"We don't know. And besides – " He thought for a moment, running his fingers down the side of the lemonade jug, making snake lines in the condensation.

"It's him, I just know, it's got to be," Ruby growled.

"Thing is, the thing is – "

"What thing?" Ruby almost stamped her foot. Why couldn't he see?

"Steady on, Rubes." He jerked his head towards the door. "It might cause trouble."

"Oby's goat being murdered by that bloody horrible Stan is trouble."

"No need to swear, is there?"

She threw him a look.

"If it was him – "

"If it was him," Ruby scoffed.

"Yes, I know it most likely was. But we've got no proof and everyone round here is going to believe Stan. No one really likes Oby and his lot. Do they?"

Ruby knew it was true.

"And there's the bird."

"He killed her as well, bet he did. He's a nasty man."

"He is nasty, Ruby. I'm not arguing, but if we start telling the grown-ups all this, there's going to be – " He thought and stared out of the window, he could see Oby walking down the back path, towards the stile.

"Well, they might find out about Gabriel and everything. See?"

She did, of course it was plain as day. She hadn't thought about that, just how Stan deserved to be caught, going round killing things like that, just for the sake of it. Didn't make sense. When her dad killed birds or rabbits it was food, that was the only reason and that was normal. Not this, this wasn't right. Stan gave her the shivers.

"See?" Peter turned to face her.

"Yes, I s'pose," Ruby sighed. "What should we do, then?"

"Don't know."

"We can't do nothing. He's a murderer!"

"Come on, Rubes. That's a bit dramatic."

"Well, he is, I think, anyway."

"We should keep an eye on him, maybe." Peter gave her a careful look, she got caught in ideas so fast. It was tricky. Look at this plane stuff, she was only going to be disappointed, he'd seen it before. Gabriel wouldn't be able to take her up in the plane, that's if it ever got off the ground. There was a lot to do if that was to happen.

"Where he's going?" Ruby had just noticed Oby, at the stile now, climbing up.

"Probably going to meet his aunty," Peter stared after them, "down on the bottom road."

"Come on then!" Ruby was already by the door.

In the wood

Gabriel had found the hollow tree some years before, but not taken much heed of it, only as a curiosity perhaps and another of the many echoes from his childhood. He and his sister had once lived in a house with a hollow tree at the edge of the garden, just where a small brook ran and where he'd caught his first tiddler when he was six. They'd played there endlessly, him using it as a hideout and her trying to turn it into a small house, bringing her dolls and other cluttering, homely objects. When he was nine, though, they had moved from that house to one on the outskirts of the town and he and his sister had complained bitterly about the loss of this precious place, but as usual none of the adults had taken any notice and move they did. Now, Gabriel smiled at the memory of it. It was an old oak, lightning struck a long time ago, he surmised, and fringing the clearing where the plane had lain hidden all this time. He dipped inside the tree, surprised again at how much space there was inside, room for someone to sleep should they choose to do so. And there was light too, but bending in at an angle from higher up the trunk, where one of the branches has long since cracked and fallen. An entry for light, but positioned so that it would have to rain very hard for water to reach the space where he now stood. He peered out, it really would make an exceedingly fine hiding place, if another were needed, for just in front was a tall mass of ferns, which masked any indication of an opening. It was something to keep in mind, he told himself, as he stepped out again into the patched and shifting mix of shadow and sunlight.

Now to business, though. He brushed the crumbs of tree from his shirt and walked towards the plane, feeling pleased that he had, for once, decided to risk coming in daylight. At night, this place filled him with such unease, almost fear. Coming here and being able to cast his eyes up to the sharp-hot summer blue, he felt sure that no dark voices would be able to break through, not on such a day.

Sitting in what remained of the cockpit, he wondered if he would be able to fly a plane if it came to it. The biggest part of the If being constructing a machine capable of lifting off the ground, the next his own ability. He had flown, but a long time ago and it was not an experience he relished; his job had been to navigate. Gabriel laughed a laugh heavy with irony and whispered the name that never left his head.

"You can do it, you know."

He swung round and stared back into the broken wreck that was mostly dark and covered with trails of ivy and other greenery, become as it was, like part of the wood itself. A strange monument to a long-ago battle. So cast off by the years now, he saw it as a story about other men, with himself a shadowy player, that's all. A bizarre idea, since he was, it would seem, still alive, where as they ...

A scene flashed at him: gunfire, heavy and lethal coming up from the ground, smoke from the tail, his name being called, bodies jumping, parachutes opening like peonies and then just the two of them and the bump of a landing across a suddenly appearing field, then into trees, miraculously still in one piece, the two of them – three, if you counted the craft itself, which had, during the years, taken on its own character. Darkness, pain, blood, but survival. Miracle was the word, the one they had both used so frequently during those first days and weeks. Until the coming of winter when healing stopped and bitterness took root and began to grow.

"I thought we were fighting for the same things, old friend. Remember? Those nights of talking – "

"- and drinking," Gabriel whispered, allowing himself a thin smile.

"The stories, you were a good story teller. Those folk tales, brought to life. Remember?"

"Snow White, was always my favourite, but never yours, eh?" Gabriel nodded to himself.

"You made it something it was not," the voice reminded him. "You twisted and turned all the old stories into a stick to beat all of us. Me. Now you. Do you not see?"

"Stories are there for a purpose. I told you, they are more than themselves, they are for teaching us how to live, and – "

" – how to die?"

"Yes." The harshness of his own voice sprang at him.

"But Snow White, for my God's sake! That drivel about it mirroring our homeland. Pah!"

"But it is true," Gabriel found a familiar fervour. "Do you not see?"

"It is just a story of an older woman's jealousy of a younger and more beautiful girl. That is all."

"Jealousy is correct. It can destroy; it has destroyed."

"A story, Gabriel, that is all. A story of vanity over-reaching itself."

"Exactly," Gabriel murmured quietly now. "So, tell me how did this happen? Huh?"

"A handsome prince from far away came and rescued Snow White, they were married and lived happily ever after. Every child knows this!"

"A prince from another land, that is so. And the old queen?"

"She – now let me see – ah, I have it. She was forced to wear some red-hot shoes made of iron and thus she danced herself to death. You see, I do know it"

"Exactly so," Gabriel sighed, his vision back as he registered the empty gloom of the plane. "She danced herself to death."

Gabriel shook himself back from the past, alone once more.

The farm

It was Sunday morning and Ruby was sitting on the swing, to and fro, to and fro, trailing her toes in the still damp grass, waiting for Peter to come round so they could, at last, go and find Gabriel, take him the book, make plans. Peter had said that he'd surely have to get the plane built, or at least make a good start, before winter. The sun was already warm and the back door was open and she could hear her mum and dad, he was going down to the oast later to check over stuff there. Hop picking would be starting a week on Monday.

"Queer, though," Mum was saying.

"Yes, but Stan was always a funny one," her dad answered.

Ruby pricked her ears.

"Hanging about round the kids, I don't like it." Her mum sounded cross now.

"What do you mean?"

"Oh, I don't know, it's just that he's always about the place. Lurking."

There was a sigh and a thump as Dad dropped one of his boots. "Doesn't do much bloody work if he can help it, that's him all over."

"Yes, he's a lazy sod. If it was up to me I'd have sacked him years ago."

"You've never forgiven him, have you?" What could her dad mean? Ruby stopped swinging and listened hard.

"No. And I never shall, either. It was a cruel thing, he did to you, and it's left its mark, on all of us."

"Come on duck." Dad was always good when you got upset. Calm and steady.

"You can't tell me you don't still feel it! What about that feather?" There was a sniff then and the sound of nose blowing. Ruby was shocked. Her mum was crying, she must be really, really upset. But what could it be that was so horrible? And what feather? They must mean that swan's feather, the one Peter had given her and her dad had chucked on the fire. She couldn't see how Stan fitted in there, though.

"There, there." Ruby could see from the shadows that Dad was hugging her mum. She wondered what to do, go in, stay where she was and pretend she hadn't heard, but just at that moment Peter appeared at the gate and waved at her. They'd both agreed that they'd have to go to the wood without telling anyone where they were going.

"What's up?"

"Don't know." Ruby slid off the swing and picked up the bag, an old canvas one they used for trips to Seashell Flats. It was the right size to hide the book from view.

"Come on." Peter kept his eyes on the back door.

"I'd better – " Ruby shrugged, not sure.

"Just call out like usual." He frowned, anxious now.

"Oh, all right." She heaved a sigh and called out, not expecting that her mum would appear so suddenly, her eyes streaked and red.

"Where are you two off now?"

"Chalk Hole," Peter said, quickly. It was their name for the pit by the caves under the Mound.

"You just be careful." Ruby turned away, she didn't like seeing her mum so tired and creased looking and it felt like her fault.

"Yes, Mum." She dashed forward and wrapped her arms round in a quick squeeze and whispered Sorry, but so softly that no one could hear.

"What's up?" Peter asked again, once they were out and off up the lane between the banks, overhung with hawthorn branches, weighed down by the mass of red berries, already lighting up the hedgerows like careless treasure.

"Mum was upset." She kicked at the dust and filled her sandals with its creamy soft warmth.

"Upset?" Like Ruby, he'd never seen Mrs Moon anything but cheerful and in charge, making everyone, including him, feel safe. "What about?"

"Don't know, but she was crying." And as she spoke a tear sprung out, followed by another and another and before long, Ruby was taking great gulps and Peter stood for a minute shrugging, eventually finding one of his amazingly clean handkerchiefs and handing it to her.

"Look," he said, steering her towards an old tree trunk just before the farm gateway. It was where they sometimes sat and planned their games.

"Sorry," Ruby sniffed, "sorry."

"P'rhaps she'd had a barney with your dad?" It happened in his house, usually ending with his mum having a good grizzle.

"No!" Ruby was shocked. "That wasn't it! Anyway, they never argue." And it was true, they never did.

"Can't think, then." He stared off down towards the oast, where he could see someone moving about on the verandah, where the hop pokes were kept in dry weather during picking. He sighed; they'd be back at school soon.

They sat for a while and Peter whistled a gentle tune, Westering Home, one of his favourites and one of Ruby's too. A song from their Friday afternoon singing lesson – one of the good things about school, that was.

He looked down at her. "One of your ribbons is coming loose."

She pulled the plait round and tightened the spotted green and white ribbon with her teeth. Her hair tasted salty, she thought, like the taste of the sea wind. "It was scary," Ruby said, "Mum crying and everything. Something about Mr. Pierce."

"Oh?"

"I told you." Ruby hugged her knees.

"Told me what?"

"He's bad man and he does bad things." She set her chin and rested it on her clenched balled-up fist.

"Well." Peter was careful.

"Well what?"

"Mum says he was made that way because of the War. It – " he looked up and frowned, searching for the word, "twisted lots of people, that's what she says. He was evacuated and then he went back for the Landings at the end."

"The War!" she scoffed. "What's that got to do with it?" All the same, she gave a sudden shiver. "Wonder if he's still got his gun?" Her eyes went wide.

Peter eased himself off the low branch and stood up. "Come on, Rubes. We should go."

"See Gabriel," she said, hoiking the bag over her shoulder. "Bet he'll be excited about the book."

"Bet he will," said Peter.

And so, off they went, down through the farmyard, past the oast house, where Ruby's dad had arrived and gone into the bunk room where he saw the wisp of white in the middle of the table, stirring a little in the draught from the door, for all the world as if a bird had flown in and dropped it there.

The camp and in the wood

It had never happened to him before, the children running at him, throwing stones and calling names. They had somehow – not ignored him, exactly, but treated him as they might one of the wild creatures that lived there, acknowledging him as one of the threads of the place to which they were all connected. Except for Oby, of course, who had lately, because of the other two, Ruby and Peter, become almost a friend, as they had too. This was a good thought, in spite of the stones, one of which had struck the back of his neck that now felt tender. He guessed what the cause of this unusual attack was, they must have decided that he had killed Oby's goat, it was obvious. Obvious and sad. He wondered if Oby had also come to believe this; the boy hadn't been among the stone throwers, but that didn't mean very much. It was Saturday, after all, a day when he might visit his aunt down by the river, something Gabriel had come to know and, in a strange way, value as a piece of knowledge; a link to the warm life of another.

Gabriel was sad. Part of his life here had been lost; the peace he had found, the sense that the darkness that edged him when he was alone, could be pushed back, perhaps completely, one day. And also, the feeling that going home was at last a real and hopeful possibility, instead of the anger and distaste he had felt so intensely until quite recently. He walked back towards his cabin pondering on what he should do. Maybe this notion about the plane that, with the fired imagination of the children had started to become a serious intention, was just madness. He should leave, just pack his few belongings and start to walk, and then when he reached the sea, find a way across; there would be a way, he was sure of it. And then what? The long walk home. He shuddered, suddenly a huge weariness washed over him and he almost sank to the ground among the ferns, never to get up again, but become absorbed into the floor cover of the wood; his wood, as he realised he thought of it now. "My wood," he said aloud.

"You see", sneered the familiar voice not far behind him, "how they treat you? What do you expect, eh, my old friend? From such as these, huh?"

Gabriel stopped and spun round. The washed out filtered streaks of light sifted into the shadows where – he stared for a moment – was that a figure who had a moment ago, darted behind the ash tree to his left?

"Hello?" he called, but only the late afternoon breeze seemed to answer, rustling the tops of the trees into a low whisper of sound. He started walking again, but before he'd gone a few yards, the voice taunted him once more: "You should have left years ago, you know that, don't you? Nobody wants you here, wanted you here. Why have you stayed, are you a coward, after all? You should have let me do what was right."

"Right? To kill these innocent farmers?"

"It was war!"

"They would have come after us."

"A fire in their hop drying place, a tree on the railway line. It would have been easy, Our duty. But what did you care about that?"

Gabriel fell to his knees and covered his face with his hands which became strangely wet. He held them out and shook them and then heard the quiet sob that came from his own chest. He was crying! It was beyond belief, surely? The words of an old rhyme from childhood tipped into his memory:

Little horse do gallop
Over stick and over stones,
But don't break your legs.
Hop! Hop! Hop!
Little horse do gallop.

It was the last time he remembered crying in this way, not as a child but as a young man. He had gone to meet Anna after two years of parting, they had arranged the place by the lake where they had both played as children. It had been one of their favourite playing haunts, swimming in summer, skating in winter and making their camp among the trees on one of the banks above what they thought of, always, as their cove. War was in the air and past attachments took on a keen poignancy, people were remembering freer times and seeing old friends and lovers just in case, because you never knew. This is how the meeting had come about.

She was already there, waiting sitting on the bank in the curved-out hollow that gave shelter from the wind and where they used to plan the house they would one day build, right here by the water's side, with the mountains visible between the high roll of wooded country on the other side. It had been all play, and his friendship and later love for her had made the move to the nearby town from the fields and forests of his childhood at first bearable and then ultimately, the best part of his life at this time.

He was about to holla out the owl call hello they had made for themselves, with variations if one was trying to tell the other that someone else was there, or for those periods when Herbert came to visit, so that she would know that Gabriel was not alone. He had lifted his hands to cup to his mouth and – then he saw. She was not by herself. A child was tottering towards her holding a stone, or some such in his hands, calling, "Mama, Mama, see!" He knew at once why she had asked him to come and decided that he couldn't hear the words from her, seeing this tender scene, the child's hands outreached, Anna with her arms waiting to gather him to her and share their private delight, and he could hear her singing the rhyme to her little boy, gentle voiced with laughter running through. Gabriel felt like an intruder and so he turned and walked back along the track, before she had the chance to know that he was there and found himself, singing over and over Little horse, little horse. And then, when he was truly alone, the tears. Further along the track he had passed an old man who had stared at him with concern, gesturing his hands as if to offer help, but Gabriel just shook his head and walked blindly on, barely knowing how he had reached the road. Away, away, was all he could hold in his mind. Seeing Anna with the child, someone else's child, was almost more than he could bear.

And later, when he turned it all over in his memory, he realised how stupid he had been; of course, he had heard via mutual friends that she was with someone else – no one he knew, thankfully – therefore it should have been obvious that she might have a child, for she had always said how much she wanted children, at least five. She'd laughed and he'd teased her, nurturing the half-formed picture in his mind of all of them cramming into his car to visit the lake, and their cove, Anna setting out the picnic on the shore, while he taught them to swim, skate, fish, according to the season, because that's what fathers did.

Instead, he never visited the lake again and tried to push even the notion of it as a real place, far from his mind, like a hurt that we bury for fear that by acknowledging its existence it will have the power to injure us again and again, and with even greater harshness.

"How alone you are!" Gabriel heard the words and suddenly shook himself up from the mulched floor of the wood, taking a moment to realise that it was his own voice. That was all. No other. The echo that had re-awakened this memory had, for the time being, gone, and only the soft sounds of the wood, the birds and the distant whistle of a train on its way to London, or the coast, broke into the gathered stillness of the late afternoon.

He could also hear the thud, thud of beating close by, drumming loud. Holding his breath he recognised that what he had heard was simply the beating of his heart, empty and shattered as it was; his heart.

Later, back in his hut, he suddenly felt chilled, and yet the oven heat of the day, of all the days of the summer, meant that usually even here, in his half-hidden clearing, the warmth stayed until late into the evening. He wrapped himself in his greatcoat and beat his arms across his chest, but it was no use. He would have to lie down. Sleep, that would be the best answer and soon; so, as the nightingales that visited this part of the wood began to scatter out their songs to one another in the dusky air, Gabriel slept.

The camp

Peter hadn't wanted to come to Oby's camp first, there were times when he just longed for it to be as it always had, before this summer, before Gabriel and Oby. But – well – it was no use minding or making a fuss, Ruby usually got her own way and mostly, it was his way too. She said she needed to collect her wings; the swan's wings that had been the cause of so much of the trouble (was it trouble?) had got left behind and both of them thought it must have been when they got to Oby's.

"What d'you want them for, anyway?" Peter sat on the gate to the now empty goat pen. Since Nancy's death the goats had been moved down to the other camp by the river, where Mina lived and where it was felt to be safer to let animals roam free in the lush meadows and in sight of everyone.

"They're mine," she said, thinking but not saying, how when her plaster came off, well, then she'd get climbing again. Best not to say that to Peter, though. He might try and stop her because of last time.

"Yeah, but – " He frowned down at her. "Your mum won't like it, or your dad." Peter remembered the earful he'd got after the accident. He'd found the wings, he'd shaped them to fit Ruby, it was all his fault. That's how he felt and he'd been relieved that Ruby seemed to have forgotten all that flying stuff – apart from the plane, but that was different, that would be real flying, not all the fairy/angel ideas that Ruby seemed to have swilling about in her head.

"Who's going to tell them?" She flashed him a glare. "We'll keep them in the caves and then no one will know."

Peter shrugged and slid off the gate: "C'mon, then, let's go and see if Oby's in."

Ruby heard the sigh, but ignored it. Those wings were important and in a way, a sort of lucky charm that would make it possible for her to fly. They really would. But when they knocked on the door of Oby's caravan there was no answer and some of the other children wouldn't say where he was, sticking out their tongues and telling them to Bugger off!

The hut in the wood

"Shush!" Peter put his hand up to Ruby. They were in the clearing near Gabriel's cabin, sun flowed through the tree tops, stirring the light into a moving net of brightness and shadow and from inside the cabin, the sound of talking.

Ruby frowned, about to speak and Peter shook his head, his fingers to his mouth. Then he signalled that they should both get down and creep slowly toward the opening that served as a window. "Quietly," he hissed at her, she was breathing too loudly, surely anyone could hear.

The talking was loud, shouting almost, and none of it made sense to them and it was soon clear that it was Gabriel, just Gabriel and no other, but so angry and upset as if he did have someone else there. Eventually, Peter lifted his head to peer in; it was hard to see at first, then he made out the sleeping form of the man stretched out on his make-shift bed, wrapped in his coat and all the time his arms waving, like he was fending off an attacker.

"He's asleep." Peter turned to Ruby and pulled a face.

She stood up properly and looked in, her mouth dropped open. What had happened? Gabriel was jabbering strangely, waving his arms, frightened, but there were two things that made her step back, suddenly afraid. "He's died!" she rasped, grabbing Peter's arm, "Look!"

"What?" He pushed her out of the way and then saw what she had seen. Wings, spread behind Gabriel's shoulders and that light circling his head, just like the pictures they had up in their classroom at school of the angels.

"Archangel Gabriel," Ruby was whispering, appalled. "That's who he is. That's who." She started to giggle and dance about from one leg to the other. Afraid. It all made sense; they said when you died and went to heaven you took your place among the angels and here it was, right in front of them. So, it was true! And Blackness, had the same happened to her? She stared in at the opening again, wondering if the cat might appear, because it would only be right and surely give company to Gabriel now that he had left them.

Except he hadn't, though. It was a puzzle. If he had died and joined the angels, how come they could still see him? Were they dead too? No, that was silly.

"He's not well," Peter told her, while she was trying to work all this out in her head. "A fever," he added, "come on." He leaned on the wooden door and shoved at it. For a minute Ruby stood there amazed at his bravery, not able to speak or move.

"But," was all that would come, "but." She followed him inside.

"The wings, though." Ruby was sitting on the rough stool, stirring the hot, sweet tea that Peter had made and thrust at her to stir in the condensed milk.

"They're yours, stupid!" He sighed, she could be weird could Ruby, but this was different. She just wouldn't believe him and, as he tried to convince her he started to wonder if there wasn't something in what she was saying. He didn't think Gabriel was dead and turned into an angel, no not that, not now they were in and could see what a state he was in, burning, hot and rambling, using all those funny words, like a spell, or a song. Ill, a cold, flu probably. You could still get that, even in summer, he knew. Yes, Gabriel was definitely different from anyone else he'd ever come across. It wasn't just that he lived out here, in the wood. Bodgers, the men who made chairs and stools and other bits of everyday furniture, they often came and stayed among the woods for a whole summer season, but Gabriel wasn't like them, he didn't make things, at least not to sell, or for a living. And then there was the way he talked, and now, all this – perhaps he really was a Ghost Man, the one everyone had been talking about for years, the one who stole things and who would steal children, especially if they were naughty, least that's what some people said. Not an angel, but like one, maybe. Peter wondered if they should go and fetch someone. Oby's mum? That wasn't a good idea, perhaps, judging by the kids who'd shouted at them and, anyway, she was probably down at the river site with Oby visiting her sister, Mina.

So, what to do?

"He is from up there, though," Ruby was staring at Gabriel

and nodding her head, as if certain of one thing. She held the tin cup carefully, taking in the sweet smell of the steam, wondering how they would get him to drink it.

"Up where?" Peter was cross, he was the one in charge and he didn't know what he was supposed to be doing.

"The sky," Ruby said, "I know he is. You can tell."

Peter snorted, "Oh, yeah?" None of this helped. "Well, wherever he's from, he's not well and we've got to help him. All right?" It was no good getting cross with her when she was in this mood, away with the fairies, his mum called it because Ruby was known for being a bit over-imaginative.

"He is." There was no arguing.

"Give us that." He took hold of the cup, but she wouldn't let go.

"No, I'll do it." She leaned forwards and gently touched Gabriel's lips with the cup's edge. "Tea, tea," she said, "Peter made it for you and I put the milk in." It was all held in a moment and then, he opened his eyes, blinking at both of them as if they, not him, were the strangers.

"It'll do you good," encouraged Peter.

"D- thank you," Gabriel's voice came out from deep in his chest, muffled and harsh, as if it had forgotten what it was for.

"I'll hold it." Ruby knelt next to him putting the cup to his lips, while Peter held his head forwards because it was obvious he couldn't manage it for himself.

And after finishing the tea, Gabriel slowly sat up, his coat still wrapped tightly about him as if he was cold, in spite of the growing warmth of the morning. He shuddered too, for a moment, making Ruby and Peter step backwards because he really did look a bit like Funny Frank, who on the weekends when he was allowed out of hospital to visit his mother, wandered the lanes of the farm muttering into the hedgerows. He was – in truth – more scared of others than they need be of him, but the children most of all never swallowed that. Gabriel, though, looked wilder and gone further from them than they had ever seen, his eyes looking at them, but not really seeing them. Ruby was the first to step forwards and quickly touch his shoulder where, strangely, the wings – her wings – had become jammed into the folds of his coat. "Peter says you've got a fever," she told him, "and p'raps we ought to get the doctor to – "

Gabriel grabbed her then tugging her towards him in a hard and surprising movement, making her gasp.

"No doctor! No doctor! You understand me, yes?"

"Yes, yes," she shook her head, trying unsuccessfully to pull away from him, "I mean no, we shan't get the doctor, honest."

He let her go then, and sank back, closing his eyes. Ruby stepped away from him and whispered to Peter: "He's worried because of coming from up there I expect." Again she jerked her head towards the sky.

"Well, maybe," Peter was beginning to think she might be right. Gabriel, when he thought about it, was so different from anyone else they knew. Really, the way he spoke, how he moved, how he looked – so much taller than any of the people they knew. And the plane, from what Oby had told them, it was a mess, if he had come in that, well, didn't it make sense, if he hadn't been killed, well surely that was some sort of miracle in itself. Miracle, or magic. There was something else too: who was this Herbert he'd been calling for when they'd first got here and he was tossing and rolling, calling the bloke's name over and over, with lots of other words they couldn't make out?

Peter had been thinking recently how Gabriel sounded like he could almost have been a soldier from one of those films on the television. Funny that, but he knew it was a daft idea, because they were always nasty, angry blokes, wearing army uniforms and carrying guns. Gabriel was kind and gentle, look how he'd helped Ruby that time. It was only because he was ill that he shouted, but all the same, there was the business of the plane that was probably from the War. No, stupid, it was too long ago and the enemy had been defeated and lived in their own country, not this one.

"We should get more water," Ruby was saying, "to cool him down. Feel." She had her hand on Gabriel's forehead which was sticky with clammy sweat.

"I'll go." Peter slid off the stool and searched around for the bucket Gabriel used to collect water from the well or the spring that came out of a sloping rocky piece of ground just a little way from the hut. The water was always cold, no matter how hot the weather, and had a sharp, not unpleasant peaty taste. It was one of a number of places in this wood where springs appeared, all to do with those wells they reckoned.

He turned as he ducked through the door opening. "You be all right here?"

"Yes," she told him, "he won't hurt me." They both knew this was true ordinarily, but Peter was still unsure; he came back and stared at Gabriel for a minute. He was quieter now, sleeping a little more peacefully and with only an occasional twitch of his arms as a dream caught him. "OK. Shan't be long."

Once Peter had gone, Ruby started singing, just as she did whenever she had the chance when she was on her own. A low hum at first and then the words of one of her favourites:

> My Bonnie lies over the ocean
> My Bonnie lies over the sea,
> My Bonnie lies over the ocean,
> Oh bring back my Bonnie to me!
> Bring back, bring back
> Oh bring back my Bonnie to me, to me,
> Bring back, bring back
> Oh bring back my Bonnie to me.

"You are Ruby." Gabriel had opened his eyes and was staring at her.

"That's right," she said. "You feeling better?"

"Ruby," he said again, shaking his head slowly. "Not her, not my own girl." His voice was thick with the struggle of speaking.

"No." Ruby didn't know what he meant.

"Sing your song again, I have heard it before."

Ruby began, less sure now, nervous that she might get it wrong, when it seemed important not to.

"There," he sighed, when she'd finished, "Anna must be so proud of you, yes?"

"Anna who?"

"My own girl," he said, "your mother." And then something else that Ruby couldn't catch.

"My mum's name is Margaret," Ruby told him.

"Mar-gar-ret." He twisted the word slowly, as if it was a stone he just picked up.

"That's right," she said, "and my dad's Charlie. Charlie Moon."

Gabriel laughed, as if she was the one being strange, "No, no. Herbert." He sat up and grabbed her once more, his breath smelt sour and Ruby snatched away from him. Afraid.

"Lie still," she bossed, "Peter's coming soon with water. It'll do you good. And later I've got something to show you." She tapped the book in her satchel.

"Herbert!" he insisted, "I see him. Look!" Gabriel jerked forwards and held up a shaking finger at the window opening. "Be careful! He means you harm. All of you!"

"There's nobody – " Ruby began, twisting round, but as she turned she saw him, the man, peering for a moment and then darting off and away out of sight as if he'd never been there at all.

The hopper huts

"We'll get into trouble," Peter repeated.

Ruby glowered at him. It had been her idea this, to come and raid the Red Cross box in the First Aid hut. It had just been re-stocked in time for picking which was due to start on Tuesday. "There'll be aspirins and stuff," she said, "and a proper plaster for his neck."

Once Peter had come back with the water for Gabriel, who'd drunk as if he'd never stop, they'd seen the blood on the back of his head, where the stone had carved its gash, and Ruby said it looked septic and the only thing for it was to find Dettol and anything else that might help. Peter suggested the Oast again, but that was just too tricky because the men were most likely in there, sorting out things for Tuesday.

"What about that bloke you saw?" He was pushing at the door to the hut, but it seemed to be jammed.

"Herbert," she said, "that's what Gabriel called him."

"Well, I never saw him."

"He most likely went the other way, then." Ruby could feel that Peter thought she was just making it up.

"And you shouldn't have left the book there either." It was because he was cross he was saying things like this; normally he'd just go along with her.

"Come on," she shoved at him, "make room and I'll push."

Together they opened the door and went in, finding the box and helping themselves to some of the things. It had been Peter who said that if they only took what they needed for Gabriel, maybe no one would notice there was anything missing. After all, the hoppers were known for nicking stuff, weren't they?

Luckily, Ruby had stuffed it into her satchel, because as they came round the corner of the hut, just next to the cookhouse, they saw him.

"Bloody hell," Ruby muttered and Peter jabbed her with his elbow.

"So," Stan pulled his dead fag from his mouth and slid it behind his ear, "what you two up to, eh?"

"Nothing," and even though Ruby was feeling suddenly brave and cheeky, she still had the sensation of wanting to run away when she saw Stan, the way he grinned without smiling and his eyes jabbed at you as if he knew just what you were thinking.

"Looking for someone," Peter said, knowing that Stan would need to hear something and if they could come up with a good enough story, then he'd leave them alone.

Stan leant against the pile of logs next to the Cooking Hut and grinned a slow smirk at them, pushing back his cap as if he was ready to stand there for hours.

Ruby tried hard to remember what Peter had been saying the day before, about Stan and the War, but it was a tussle because her stomach was telling her something else altogether about him.

"So," he said slowly making the word whistle through his teeth, "who would that be now?"

"Who?" Ruby jumped.

"Oby," Peter blurted it out in a rush.

"Now, I remember him" (the way Stan said him made it seem like a dirty word, somehow) "saying he was going down to their camp by the river to see that aunty of his. If I'm not wrong." He was never wrong, is what this last meant.

"Yes, we know." Peter was signalling with his hands to Ruby behind his back, telling her to leave it to him. "He's coming back this way, that's what we fixed."

"I see," Stan said, who seemed to see all too clearly.

"So," Peter shrugged and put his hands in his pockets, leaning back against one of the hut posts, with Ruby doing the same, as if they were just waiting for Oby to appear and for Stan to disappear.

For a moment no one spoke and the only sound was the sheep in High Bank Field just above where they were, tugging at the summer dried grass and chomping on it while they stared without curiosity at the three below. And in the distance a tractor droning in one of the apple orchards, taking another load to the cold store, most likely.

"See you, then, Mr. Pierce." Ruby was bold now she'd had a chance to get her breath, pushing away the idea that he might be able to see right through her bag and know exactly what they were up to. She knew that he must never find out about Gabriel; she didn't understand why this thought that was hardly a real thought, had sprung into her head, but it was strong, like having to hold on tight when you were climbing a tree and you – for a second or two – lost the sure footing you'd had for the blink of a moment before.

"Yes, we'll let you get on then," Peter said.

Stan, though, didn't show any signs of going. In fact he settled himself a little more comfortably on the wood pile and started to roll another paper and tip tobacco from his pouch, as if they were all enjoying a good old natter. Peter made a show of checking his watch.

"I'm not sure he's coming, you know," he said to Ruby.

"What?" She'd been momentarily off and away, forgetting their story already. He kicked her ankle. "Oh, Oby. No. Maybe we should go up to the camp then?" She squinted at him in the bright afternoon sunlight and smiled, it made him feel better.

"Come on, Rubes." Peter nodded at Stan.

"I'm coming that way too," was what he said and the two of them hardly dared look at one another. "And let me carry that bag for you, Ruby Moon, eh? I can tell it's heavy and you with your arm still a bit dicky, like." Within half a minute he had slid off the wood pile and was strolling along with them, carrying Ruby's bag and Ruby all of a shiver inside, in case he for some reason opened her satchel, or it came undone and the stolen contents spilled out their guilt right under his nose.

Mostly Stan talked, on and on about what he'd done in the War. "You'd think he'd won it on his own," Peter whispered to her, making her cough back a giggle, as they walked along and up past the next set of huts where already some of the Londoners were unloading their luggage, shouting out Hallos and Lovely weather for it to the three of them, as if they might be a family on a Sunday afternoon outing. "New lot," Stan muttered to them, waving cheerily, "bleedin' townies won't have a clue about anything, you watch."

"They talk funny, don't they," Ruby said, for something to say and because it was true. Not funny, like Gabriel, she thought, but funny all the same.

"They're not the only ones, eh, duck?" He gave her a sly smile. Was he a mind reader? Had he seen right into her head and now, because of her, knew all about Gabriel? If he had he'd tell, he definitely would. And then what? Her dad would be cross, really cross; he didn't set many limits on what she and Peter got up to in the holidays, but one rule about the wood, was no getting involved with strangers in there, because tramps and all sorts passed through that wild edge of the farm and you never knew who they might be. Once, too, before Ruby was born, so the story went, there'd been a murder in there and neither the murderer nor the victim had ever been found. Yet, someone had seen it happen, heard the shot and seen it, but from too far away to do anything about it. When she asked her dad about it all he'd say was that was why they should be careful, stay on the paths and if they were going to the camp, well, that was all right, but no further. If he knew what they'd been up to these past weeks there'd be hell to pay; so he must never know.

Ruby was kicking up the dust from the track, barely seeing where they'd got to while all this was tangling and untangling in her mind. She felt Peter's hand on her arm and he was saying something to her; she stared at him. "Your dad," he was saying and pointing. She looked up, they were at the Oast already and there was her dad and some of the other blokes, outside sorting through a pile of sacks. Stan had seen them too and the expression on his face changed.

"Dad!" Ruby was running over to him, feeling safe at last. She stopped when she got to him and waited until he'd finished, when he was working that had to come first and she knew to hold back. Peter was shifting about behind her, Stan hadn't moved, but they could feel his eyes casting about over them all. Above them the swallows wheeled and dipped through the air, scooping up the insects, getting ready for their long journey south.

Ruby's bedroom

Later that night, when Ruby was getting ready for bed, she turned over all that had happened from that point on. How

Stan had, eventually walked across to the Oast, how her dad had said, No thanks they didn't need his help and he'd talk to him tomorrow. Everyone knew that Stan was always wanting to be one of the Oast Boys, as they were known, but her dad wouldn't have him. Instead he'd be driving the trailer full of hop sacks – pokes they were called – from the hop garden up to here, where they'd be spread on slatted wood of the kiln floors ready for drying. She really wanted to talk to Mum about it all: everything, Gabriel, him being ill and what should they do, the plane, Oby's goat, Stan. But she knew she mustn't, Peter had said, over and over, they couldn't tell, because if they did Gabriel might get into trouble too; instead it boiled away inside her, so that by the time Mum came to tuck her and say goodnight, Ruby's face was creased and flushed with fretting.

"What's up?" her mum asked, sitting down on the edge of the bed.

"Nothing, not really." Safe and comfortable in bed now, Ruby wondered what harm it would do if she told her mum just some of it. She took a breath. From here she could see the last fierce pink of the sunset draining away behind the cherry orchard; beyond that was the oast house and further still, thick and dark, was Bower Wood.

"So, do you want to tell me about the nothing-not-really, then?" Her mum's voice was quiet, soft as a hum.

"Thing is, I promised." Ruby could hear her heart banging, not something she normally noticed.

"A promise, eh?"

"Yes." That was better, it was nearly as good as telling her mum, without actually saying the words, at least in Ruby's mind.

"It's nothing you wouldn't tell me if you could, then?"

"Oh, no. No! It's because," Ruby searched for the right way to put it, "if we tell, someone might get into trouble."

"Would the someone be Oby, by any chance?"

"Oby? No!" She clapped her hand over her mouth. Peter was forever telling her that keeping quiet was often better than actually saying too much. He'd learned that much from his mum and dad, who – according to other people – were described as keeping themselves to themselves.

"Ah, I see," Mum said, brushing a stray hair from Ruby's eyes.

Suddenly very weary, Ruby scrunched herself down under her blankets, burying her nose into her old bear and wishing she could say what it was and ask Mum what they should do. All that business with Stan and seeing her dad had meant that they really hadn't had time to go and see Gabriel and take the medicine box.

"The medicine box!"

"The what, duck?" Mum had been about to go back downstairs.

"My satchel," Ruby said, which wasn't a lie. But the awful truth settled on her. Stan had gone off with her satchel, worst of all, if he looked inside he'd know what they'd been doing down at the huts and would tell her dad. Peter. If only she could go round and tell him – now. He'd know what to do, or what to say to make her feel better. And he'd think of a way of getting it back. Oh, what a worry. Supposing Stan worked out what they were doing with the First Aid Box and would somehow magically know about Gabriel. No, that was silly, she breathed into Archie Bear again. Silly, silly. But supposing.

"That's a lot of sighing."

"Sorry Mum. I'm all right. I'll go to sleep now."

"What about your satchel?"

"I – left it somewhere."

"I hope you're being truthful, Ruby."

"Yes." She gulped as quietly as she could manage.

"Usually the best in the end, I reckon."

"Yes," Ruby felt a tear slide down her cheek. It was too hard this, not being able to talk to her mum, not being able to go back to Gabriel, when he could, for all they knew, be dying from a horrible fever and it would be their fault. They'd said they'd go back and help him and they hadn't. It wasn't fair. And letting Stan walk off with her satchel like that, seeing him hook it on the inside of the oast door as if it didn't matter and then her forgetting all about it. Peter would be cross with her when he found out. Ah, but here on the fringes of sleep, it came to her. Perhaps there was a way of not having to tell him. If she could get it back, he'd never have to know, because he'd blame her, she knew he would.

Every morning just before four, Mum went downstairs to check the range and Ruby woke up too, if her door was ajar. It was a good plan.

In the wood

Night's depths and he was dreaming of flying, remembering those times when the stars were close companions and Herbert called out their names and later, when they were home again, told stories of the heroes patterned in the constellations, whom time and fate had caught and fixed there in the vast blackness. Gabriel dreamt he was striding among them all, wings on his back to lift him above the earth. And there it was below him, his home, at first as he knew it during boyhood, awash with light and warmth, the love of his parents, the shared games with his sister, the games with Herbert, swimming, climbing and bicycling in the school holidays, and later those moments with Anna in their cove. As the pictures flickered past, he could see himself from that time too and yet here he was also, a winged and removed observer from another place, wanting to reach down and touch them all, to call out their names and hear them call his in reply.

Yet, in a sudden, painful shift the picture changed; all was altered, the houses from his home town no longer recognizable, faces contorted with anger and pain, a stumbling crowd, lost and anxious picked its way through piles of rubble and where there was once a park, barbed wire, men in uniforms and fierce dogs straining forwards, their eyes cold and soulless as gunmetal. Everywhere, too, the stinging smell of burning souring the air. Friends from school seemed to peer up towards him, glowering and waving him off, some shaking their fists as if he was the terrible visiting angel who had caused this ferocious alteration. Then as he held his hands towards them they cowered, covering their heads in fear and when he looked at his hand he saw why; he was grasping a huge black sword, as if ready to strike a swathe of death through them all. What shocked him was that he was ready to do this without a moment's more hesitation, even though his family and friends were there too with a terrible beseeching anguish written on their faces. Only Anna, stood to one side, her child's head buried in her skirt, a hazed flow of soft silvery light separating her out from the dark horror of the rest, that and her calm, yet intensely sorrowful smile.

"Anna!" As Gabriel called her name, so he awoke, slimed with the sweat from his fever, his head throbbing and his tongue gritty and dry, too large for his mouth. He stumbled from his bed – he must get to the spring, find water. He had to find water. It was as he fell, he realised that he had tripped over the full bucket left there by Peter earlier.

The farm and the oast

Ruby had been so careful, letting herself out of the back door, lowering the latch with her fingers so it didn't do its usual rattling click. Floss the dog raised her head and whined a soft good morning, but she knew who it was and didn't bark and the geese, luckily, were nowhere to be seen in the cherry orchard. Past the chicken house, past the piggery, where soon Peter's dad would be for the early morning feeding, past the farmhouse, where one light glowed upstairs, most likely the farmer's baby was awake. It was only as she passed the tar pit she got a sudden flash of fear; she always swerved as far as she could, away from this place, it looked like the hell they'd been told about at school, black and sticky, ready to suck you in if you didn't watch out.

Once she reached the oast she felt a little better, it was a bit like the church in the village, familiar, dusty and safe. "Easy," she whispered into still hop-scented dark, "don't be scared. It's all right now." And she began humming to herself, because she had the idea that should anyone be about, they'd most likely think there were two of them and leave them be. She pushed back the door and reached for the hook where Stan had idly tossed her satchel.

Nothing there!

"You looking for this?"

Ruby swung round and sighed with relief. For a minute she hadn't been able to work out who it was even though the voice was so familiar. "Oby," she breathed, leaning back against the door. "What you doing here?"

"Fetching this." In the fattening glow of dawn she made out the Red Cross box from the bunk room, "and then I saw your satchel and thought you'd want me to bring it, in case it got lost. You are always forgetting it." It was true, Ruby often left it in the cloakroom at school and it was usually Oby who offered to run back and collect it for her.

"You'd better put it back, Oby," she warned, nodding at the box, "Dad'll be down later and he'll know."

"You would tell him?" Oby frowned at her.

"No, but he'd know and most likely your lot would get the blame – or them Londoners, I suppose," she added, because once the pickers arrived things did seem to go missing and the gypsies got a rest from the blame for a while and even the Ghost Man got pushed to the back of people's minds too.

"Yes, well, I don't care, tell if you want," he challenged.

"No, you don't get it," Ruby said, knowing that she'd upset him, he could be touchy sometimes could Oby.

He tried to push by her to open the door. "It doesn't matter, anyway, I have to take this to Gabriel, he is hurt."

"I know," sighed Ruby, "that's why I'm here too."

"You are? How did you know?" He thought for a minute and nodded, "Of course, it's how the water was there, you must have got it for him."

"Well, Peter did," she said, not wanting to steal the praise. "Listen – " But both of them started, footsteps getting nearer. Too late to leave by the door, so Ruby jerked her head back towards the bunk room and within half a minute they were both wedged under the table, squeezed in amongst the rickety assortment of chairs, cast-offs, mostly, from the farmer's kitchen.

Whoever it was seemed to be looking for something near the door, but soon gave up and headed into the bunkroom. Ruby squashed close to Oby and scrunched her eyes closed. Did he (they could see his boots) know they were there and had he come for them? Ruby felt a tickle growing in her throat and swallowed hard to stop it turning to a cough; Oby gripped her arm tightly. The man was so close if they'd wanted to they could have reached forwards and tugged at his trouser legs. He stood still, breathing hard now as if he was angry and then slammed the top of the table before heading back out into the early morning. Leaving it for as long as felt safe, the two stayed under the table until they were sure the oast had that comfortable emptied feel again; just them and the waiting building – waiting for her dad and the others and for the start of hoppin' – the reason it was there, like a palace waiting for the king to arrive back from his travels. Scrabbling out from amongst the chair legs it was Oby who spotted it first, picking it up and turning it over in his hand. He frowned at Ruby, "What is this for?"

At first she thought it was from her wings, but how could it be? They were still in Gabriel's cabin because he needed them now, Ruby had convinced herself that her wings had a sort of magic about them; everyone knew that swans were special, there was that story about the seven brothers which she couldn't quite remember, but anyway the wings meant Gabriel would be able to fly back home; he would make the plane work and she would fly too, somehow.

"Why would the man leave it here like this?" Oby asked, picking it up and smoothing the white feather between his fingers. The feather had very deliberately been weighted down by a piece of flint right in the middle of the table.

"A kind of joke, I expect," she said. It seemed the only answer; the men in the oast often had a laugh with one another, writing things in chalk on the walls and drawing pictures which made them all laugh, although she could never see what was so funny about them and neither could Peter, or so he said.

"It doesn't seem funny," Oby said, putting it back under the stone.

"No," said Ruby, shrugging, and as they both stepped out into the pink light of morning, a half-remembered thought skittered away from her and dropped into forgetfulness.

Now Oby had the box he said he'd take it to Gabriel and give him some medicine and that his aunty had some herbs that would help with the wound too. He decided not to tell Ruby that Gabriel had fallen over and how he'd found him sprawled half in and half out of the doorway with blood seeping from the re-opened gash. He had managed to get him back onto his bed and given him water and made him as comfortable as he could, when he remembered the First Aid Box that Peter had fetched after Ruby's fall from the tree, which is why he'd been here.

"Best if you go back home," he smiled, showing his neat row of bright rabbit teeth shining white in his olive face. Ruby thought he looked almost pretty when he smiled like this and couldn't help agreeing and smiling back. He was right, she must go home before her Mum got up for the second time this morning to do the breakfasts.

In the wood

He had dreamt again of home and the death he might find there. Mixed in were those terrifying pictures that sprang at him, but always in black and white, only ever in black and white. Faded scenes torn at the edge, ripped from a newspaper is what some part of him surmised, because that was where he had first seen them. All those faces gripped against the wire, staring with a hollow almost inhuman solitude, faces emptied of emotion for fear of the exposure it would bring. Or perhaps it was simply that these vestiges of life were on the tipping point of starvation, not merely from lack of food, but from any – even the smallest – act of kindness from another.

Gabriel twisted his body upright halfway through a shout, yet as soon as he was awake, properly this time, he couldn't recall what he had been trying to say, only that he was burning with a fierce anger. He pulled his hand across his forehead and it came away plastered with sweat. He knew that he needed aspirin to get this temperature down, but how was that to be achieved? Water, water was the next best thing. As he eased himself off his bed and tried to stand he realised how difficult it was going to be to make the short distance to his spring. His spring, how possessive he had become of this wild and alien place, now his home. He leaned forwards trying to reach for his bucket and as he grabbed it with shaking hands he saw that it was full. How could that be? Someone had been while he had been drowning in his feverish sleep and done this kind thing.

"Herbert?" His voice came in a low weak rasp that hardly sounded like his own. "Herbert?" Gabriel called again when there was no answer. Silence still and logic told him that it could not have possibly been Herbert. Could not have possibly been.

Through the square hole that he called his window, he could see that the day was already beginning to brighten as pink stripes of sun stranded in between the trees. Another hot day in this summer of endless blue skies and warm-bathed air. A kind of blessing, Gabriel thought, since it might well be his last here. He took a deep draught of water. How good it tasted and soothing to his throat which felt gritty and rough. He drank some more and was so intent on the luxury of this simple task that he didn't hear the door being pushed open.

"You are like an angel," he told Oby as they sat, him feeding himself the aspirin and the boy having fetched yet more water, now brewing his can to make tea.

"That's what Ruby calls you," Oby told him, which wasn't

strictly true, but was the only way he could find to describe it.

"I do not understand," Gabriel said, already feeling better because he had been able to take control again, the fever had pushed him back to a childhood self, where nightmares filled his senses and robbed him of his innate self-belief that all would be well. It was something he had learnt from his mother. All would be well. She had said that when war was in its early brewing stage, but on that one she had been wrong.

"You came from up there," Oby pointed at the sky and looked to one side a little shyly in that way that he had.

"Ah," sighed Gabriel, smiling, "of course, I see."

"She's mad about flying," Oby explained, as if Gabriel might not yet have caught on to that.

"Yes, I know."

"She thinks you'll take her when you go." Oby eyed him with a careful glance.

"When I – ?" Gabriel wondered if his head was too fuzzed for this.

"The plane." Oby nodded at the book that Ruby had left and which Gabriel hadn't noticed until now.

"Yes, yes, I remember this – the plane," he laughed to himself and muttered a word that Oby didn't catch. He flicked through the book. "It is a charming notion."

"We'll help," Oby said.

"I know," Gabriel sighed and put the book down carefully, as if it had been a precious thing, like a baby animal or bird. It pleased Oby because it made him surer than ever that it couldn't have been Gabriel who had harmed Nancy in that brutal way.

"Honest, we will." Oby's eyes were shining, bright as marbles in the soft gloom of the cabin.

Gabriel drank the tea that Oby had made and looked at him steadily. How true these children were to him, such faith and yet if they knew, truly knew what kind of man he was – no, he pushed the thought back into its dark hiding place, that was no longer important. He was as he was now, and as they were making him. From the moment he'd found Ruby at the bottom of the tree he had changed and become the man he was before all the horror that had trapped the world for those few, terrifying years.

"My uncle has lots of wood and canvas, things you might use," Oby continued, "Aunty Mina's husband?" As if Gabriel might know. "He doesn't need it all and we can help."

"You have not told your uncle?"

Oby shook his head.

"Nor your aunt?"

"No, nobody," Oby clenched his hands together. "Honest."

"Of course," Gabriel sank back with relief, "you would not tell, none of you." He seemed to be speaking half to himself now.

"How you feeling?" Oby asked, afraid to talk about the plane for the moment. He wondered if it was his fault. Hadn't he been the one to suggest it in the first place?

"A little more myself, yes, thank you. And thank you for bringing these things. I hope it will not cause trouble for you?"

"No, no, Ruby helped and she'll come later and take back what you don't use. She said."

Gabriel picked up the book again, studying it with more seriousness this time.

After a minute while Oby sat quietly, much as he would when watching a rabbit in the sight of his catapult, Gabriel lifted his head from his reading and nodded at him: "We shall try it," he said, "who knows, maybe it will work and I shall find my way home and it will be because of you."

"And Ruby and Peter." Oby rated fairness very highly, suffering from so much unfairness himself.

"Of course," Gabriel agreed, "Peter and Ruby." As he said their names, he pictured Ruby, smiling and eager, arms spread falling from the tree. Was there a way he could help her to get her wish? He would have to think about this, it might just be possible.

Later as he watched Oby moving through the trees quickly blending in the way he always did, treading so lightly he hardly ruffled the undergrowth, Gabriel experienced a renewed wash of gratitude towards these children and for the first time in a long while, he felt there might, after all, be a reason to hope again.

The caves

It had been Peter's idea. They'd managed to get hold of some of the canvas that Oby's uncle had, back in his van when he was visiting the Bower Wood site. Oby had spun some story about them wanting to make a tent to camp out in while the weather still held, it had been so easy. The problem then, was where to keep it until they could get it to Gabriel and so, when Peter said the caves, Oby had been relieved. He'd been afraid that if it had been left lying around some of the other kids would be snitching bits before too long and they were going to need all they could lay their hands on, that was certain. Ruby said she thought the caves were a magic place because it really did seem that they were only ones who went into them; it was as if they'd slipped from everyone else's memory. Even Mum had mostly forgotten they were there, somehow, which was strange because years before when Ruby had just started school, they'd sometimes come here together, picking blackberries and shouting down into the hollow tubes of dark that led into the smaller caves. It was where Ruby had first learnt how to call to her own voice, catching it as it bowled back from under the earth. "That was magic," she'd said and so it stayed.

"Only thing is," Peter said, as they hauled the second sheet into the next to smallest cave, for safety he'd reckoned, "we're going to have to work out how to get it back to Gabriel without anyone noticing."

"Going to be hard with all the hoppers about." Oby scratched his ear, thinking. It was true, more of the Londoners had been arriving and now, the day before picking was due to start proper, there were crowds tramping about the farm tracks to and from the huts to the little shed on the farm that opened as a shop for hop-picking only. That and the shop on the Leas, as well as the

Half Moon, of course. It was like suddenly having a small town where before there'd only been empty lanes and the distant hum of tractors working beyond the hedges, or the call of sheep, all familiar noises that belonged. These invaders filled the air with their too loud, nervous laughter and their larky London accents. Even worse, they had the habit of going where they shouldn't, either because they didn't know, or didn't care. In a few weeks, after all, they'd be gone again and who knew what would happen between now and next year?

"School starts on Thursday too," Ruby grumbled, "it's going to take forever to make the plane if we can only help him evenings and weekends."

"If we have to, we'll take it in turns," Peter said, brushing chalk from Ruby's back; best if no one knew where they'd been.

Ruby sighed; school was just going to get in the way of everything and it was going to be a lot harder. At least Gabriel was feeling better, though, thanks to Oby, but he did look different since his fever and when he was talking to them about the plans for the plane he'd suddenly stop and stare hard into the trees as if he really did see someone there. But when they followed his gaze none of them could see anyone, although once Oby reckoned he saw a shape that could have been a bloke; then again it was probably just the shifting patterns made by the breeze. Ruby said she heard a voice now and then when she was on her own with Gabriel, and it sounded like him, but wasn't. Peter shrugged at such talk, Ruby did get carried away sometimes.

"Don't worry, Rubes." He patted her arm. "It'll be all right." Really, Peter was getting excited about the whole plane building business, like one of his kits he was always making, only this time it was real. A great big plane that might actually fly. Amazing. He had to bite his tongue when he was at home not to spill the beans, forgetting that no one but the three of them and Gabriel, of course, knew about it.

"We got to find more canvas as well," Oby said, trying to work out how they'd do that because his uncle had given them as much as he was going to. "And the engine, what about that?" He stopped as they got to the stile at the edge of the Mound, leaning back and whistling softly through his teeth and staring up the hill, thinking.

"Gabriel will work it out." Ruby sounded so sure that neither of the boys was willing to disagree and, anyway, she could be right. Hadn't he managed until now, living like he did with no job, no money and all?

"C'mon," Peter said, looking at his watch, "s'nearly dinner-time and Mum's told me if I'm late again then no out to play after school this week."

They climbed over the stile, jumping down the other side and running along the high banked track that led past the apple orchard, where it forked, one leading on to the row of cottages, and the other towards the farm and the lane to the Bower Wood, which was the way Oby went. All of them promising to meet up later in the afternoon on the railway bridge.

It meant that none of them saw the man slip out from the hazel copse near the caves and dive down into the one where they had so carefully hidden the precious length of canvas.

The farm

Mum had been busy baking all morning, buns and scones for Dad and the others in the oast, she said, but there were plenty for the kids as well. Ruby wondered if she might be able to smuggle a few to Gabriel and was busy rummaging round in the larder for a bag to hide them in when she heard the gate click. Peter already? He must had have a quick dinner, usually his mum made him help clear away and everything after. She stood on tip-toe and looked out of the tiny window on to the path. Not Peter, but Oby's aunty. She heard a gentle tap at the back door and then Mum's voice, then Mina's. It had been strange how that had happened, Mum and Oby's aunty discovering that they'd known one another long ago, when they were both at school. Something Oby had said and now they were friends again, not realising how close they'd been to each other all this time. And, in some un-named way, it had changed things too, for the better.

Ruby searched a bit longer and found an old empty tin that would fit in her little canvas bag without being seen. That would do.

"There you are." Mum threw her a hard look. She knew the kids were up to something and it wasn't that she wanted to know, more that it wasn't anything they weren't supposed to be doing, because as far as she could tell, there was a lot of whispering going on that often stopped rather too nippily whenever she, or anyone else was about. "What you doing then?"

"Nothing, Mum," Ruby blurted a little too fast and she knew it. Ah, well too late.

"Kids, eh?" She winked at Mina, who'd sat down on the piano stool and was trilling the keys absently with her left hand, making a sweet soft sound, like far-off spring water.

"They're making a tent," she said, playing with her other hand now and making a real tune that Ruby recognised, but couldn't name.

"A tent?" Mum sounded hurt, or so Ruby imagined. Wasn't it just the kind of adventure she'd have been hearing all about non-stop only last summer? Now here she was on the outside.

"Joe found some old canvas for them, didn't he my love?" Mina's sharp brown eyes smiled at Ruby.

"Yes," said Ruby, carefully stowing the tin into her bag while talk of the imaginary tent went on around her and while Mum buttered some fruit scones for them all to have with their cup of tea.

"Take these out will you, Ruby?" Mum passed her some plates and knives. "I've put the old table under the apple tree, thought it'd be nice to have it out there, you can go and call for Peter if you like."

"Peter?" This wasn't part of the plan, hadn't they got to meet

Oby soon?

"That's right, we can sit and chat to Mina for a bit then, can't we? Since she's bothered to walk up specially and her Joe's been getting stuff for you. Come on."

Normally Mum let them roam, but it was as if she was cross about something. What Ruby didn't know was that Mum had been sitting up in bed, reading, and had seen her from the window the other morning and watched her go out, down towards the farmyard. It had put her in a real quandary too, as to whether she should try and follow, or wake Charlie. Instead, she'd dropped back into sleep and the next she knew the alarm was going off and Ruby was back in her room, as if she'd never left and the morning started like it always did.

"You going?" Mum was fussing about with jam and butter, so Ruby got up, stashing her bag behind a pile of newspapers.

"Do you need help to carry things out, Megs? You seem a bit out of sorts today," Mina was saying just as Ruby swung down the back steps in a hurry to get round to Peter's. How queer it was to hear her mum's name shortened like that, making her into another person, almost. Dad never called her Megs.

"I'll go on me own," Peter said, when she told him about Mina turning up and how she had to hang around, which twisted Ruby into a small burst of fury. She stuffed the end of one of her plaits into her mouth and chewed on it. A sure sign.

"But s'not – " she muttered through a wodge of hair.

"Listen." He dropped his voice, they were standing by Peter's front gate and his mum, like Ruby's, was busy with baking all ready for the Off, as they called it, meaning the start of picking. Everything revolved round that at the moment and it was getting in the way of their doings. "It might be better, you being here makes it like a – " He struggled for the word that he'd heard someone use in a play on the wireless that meant one person did something while the other went off to do the important business. "Decoy," he said.

Ruby, who never stayed angry for long, lifted her shoulders and shrugged, knowing he was right. What mattered was getting the canvas to Gabriel and they'd agreed that he'd have to help them do that, which meant going to his cabin, arranging where and when, probably after dark, (Ruby had a plan about that) and making a list of other bits he was going to need. When it came to it, whether Ruby was there or not didn't really matter. Just as Peter turned to go she remembered the scones and buns in her bag and rushed back in, nearly bumping into Mina as she came out carrying the tea cups.

"You must be careful," she said, with a smile, and later Ruby thought she might have meant something else altogether, not just tearing about not looking where she was going.

Sitting on her swing, later, full of Mum's baking and warm sweet tea, Ruby thought that it wasn't so bad being left behind. Except she was sorry not to see Gabriel, he was special to her and she thought she was to him too. Since her accident she'd been banned from climbing and swinging from high tree branches and she missed the wild whooshing of it, the nearest she got to flying, but Gabriel had promised she would fly. And she believed him. She wondered, as she sat, twirling and untwirling the rope of her swing, so when it got as tight as it could and she let go, it span round, dizzying the warm light of the afternoon into a blue-gold blur, she wondered if he was in some way magic, or a ghost, even. That time they'd got to his cabin and seen him with her wings, well, he had looked just like an angel and it was, whatever Peter said, how she still secretly thought of him. What's more before they really knew him, he was called the Ghost Man, still was by everyone else, and angels and ghosts were almost the same.

"Yes, a terrible business," Mum was saying, waving her hand at a dozy wasp that had flopped onto the now empty plate of scones.

"What was?" Ruby's ears pricked.

"The War, lovey," Mina said.

"Yes," said Ruby, who'd seen films about it, some of them, those newsreels that flickered from that long ago time, too scary to watch.

"And the first one was almost as bad." Mum sipped the last her tea and flung the dregs into the long grass.

"Oh, you should have let me look," Mina said, leaning forward and putting her arm on Mum's hand, and they both giggled, echoes of the girls they were still, somewhere inside.

"I'll see if there's any left in the pot," Mum said, "and you can next time."

"Can what?" Ruby asked, although she had an idea it was to do with the tea leaves, because Mina could read palms; in one of her comics, Ruby had seen that some people could also read the patterns left at the bottom of tea cups and tell the future that way. She was sorry she'd chucked hers away now.

While Mum was pouring, Mina started talking about the War again. "You lost your father then Megs?"

"Yes." Mum stopped for a minute and stared up through the tangle of apple branches at the patched smears of sharp blue sky. Was he up there, somewhere, Ruby wondered, her Missing Presumed Dead grandfather she'd never known?

"A good man," Mina said, flattening the folds of her tiny flowered patterned skirt. "If his daughter is anything to go by." She smiled, her face bright and vivid.

"He was," Mum said and sighed, "a rare one, as I've discovered to my cost."

"My father was killed in that one too," Mina said.

Mum nodded, Ruby knew, because she'd told her only the other day, how sad it had all been because how Mina – newly married to Joe – had lost her first baby due to the shock of it and all. A shock because her dad, at least, had come home alive at the end. But he'd been gassed, they said, and it had damaged his lungs, a dose of influenza and he was dead.

"And in this last one, well," Mina shrugged and lifted her hands, as if there were no words to tell the bigness of that story.

"You lost someone close?" Mum's voice was edged with

surprise.

"Joe's family on his mother's side were all in Hungary," Mina said, staring again at the folds of her skirt, as if there might be something hidden and secret there.

"Were?" Mum asked. "So, where are they now, then?" It was true, Ruby thought, Oby's Uncle Joe did talk different, all the gypsies did, but his words often came out crumbly, a bit like Gabriel's sometimes.

Mina looked up, frowning. "Dead."

"All of them?" Mum was shocked, Ruby could see.

"All," Mina said, almost whispering, "even the smallest baby."

"How terrible!" Mum was shaking her head and she leaned forwards and patted Mina's arm. "In the bombing, I s'pose?"

"No," said Mina, half glancing towards Ruby, and dropping her voice, "in the camps."

Mum seemed to take a minute to fathom this.

"It wasn't just – " Ruby couldn't catch all of what Mina was saying, "but us too, you know and others who were different. They tried to kill them all."

"I didn't realise." Mum sat back in her chair, staring at Mina as if she wasn't sure who she was, "I didn't realise."

"No," said Mina, "lots of people don't."

"I'm so sorry." Mum had tears in her eyes. Ruby was puzzled.

"What camps?" she said, making them both jump. They seemed to have forgotten she was there.

"Shocking," Mum was still saying.

"In the War," Mina said, gentling her voice and trying to smile again. "Lots of bad things happened."

"Yes," said Ruby, standing up on her swing seat and moving to and fro, like a trapeze artist, wondering if Mina could see how clever she was. "I know, I saw it on television."

"Those camps, though," Mum muttered, like she was talking to someone who wasn't there.

"Yes, I know," Ruby said again, "that was on one of them programmes. Lots of thin people in stripy clothes and – " she waved her hand, wanting to be like them, to say she knew all about it, so they'd let her join in properly, "barbed wire, like the pigs have to keep them in."

"The pigs, indeed," said Mina, shaking her head, "yes, just like that Ruby." She got up and ruffled Ruby's hair. "Don't worry about it, it's in the past now and everything is better."

"I'm not worried," said Ruby, who, if she'd been truthful would have admitted that she was, just a bit, that those programmes had scared her and slipped into her dreams some nights; all those scary people staring and staring through the barbed wire, all of them staring at her, like she knew something they wanted to know. And when she woke up she'd sometimes be crying, but she couldn't say why.

"Mina," Mum said, "I'm so sorry, I'd no idea. You must think I'm a daft biddy, eh?"

"Please," said Mina, waggling her eyebrows and nodding her head, ever so slightly, towards Ruby, "it wasn't your fault, you know," she tried to laugh, but Mum was still frowning, "and it's all in the past now."

"Can't forgive them, though," Mum said, "never. Killing all those poor souls like that, even the kiddies. Terrible. Unforgivable, I say."

"Forgive who?" Ruby was curious.

There was no answer as Mum and Mina had got up and started clearing away the tea things, talking about hop picking and how long the weather might hold. But Ruby guessed anyway; they meant the enemy, whose trespasses would never be forgiven.

In the wood

Gabriel stared at the plane. It was serious, this business of trying to make it fly again when he saw how broken and fragile it really was. "It's madness," he said aloud into the darkening trees, and this time there was no answering, mocking agreement from Herbert, who often seemed to be less talkative when the children were there or – as was the case now – just gone. It was as if their innocent presence pushed the blacker spirits away and for this, Gabriel was thankful. They had, he knew, brought a gentle healing to his lonely, crooked existence. Reminded of his debt to them, he began to clamber, once more, into the shell of what had brought him here, all those years before.

He had brought a pencil and some paper, supplied by Peter, and also a round metal tape-measure, because the boy, who had become alive with excitement as the plan was hatched, had said, rightly, that measuring what was needed and then cutting it in the caves, might make carrying that much easier. It also meant that Gabriel wouldn't have the problem of where to store the whole thing. Peter said it would keep dry in the caves too, which was also a good notion. He was a practical boy, Gabriel reflected, much like the son he and Anna might have dreamt off in that far-off other life. Anna; the name fell softly from his lips and gave him the courage to imagine himself going home, really going home. Even after all that had happened between him and Herbert, all the raging between them and the ultimate, terrible final scene, he now felt oddly calm about it, as if it had become a separate thing in itself. And as he measured and drew, some of those old habits of precision and careful reckoning, of wanting to do a task as well as he could, began to re-awaken and it seemed that his hands started to recall the actions required of them and the sketches started to transform into a rough, but recognisable design. The light, though, was already draining from this part of the wood, always quick to soak up the night's shadows, Gabriel decided he would finish the drawings back in his hut and have them ready to take down to the cave later. For it had been agreed that he would fetch the canvas pieces at night, to avoid any chance of being seen. It was – he smiled to himself – his familiar time for gathering his supplies and when he felt most at ease.

The Mound

Ruby knew that if she was found out there'd be big trouble; coming here after dark, once again creeping out, but she just had to come. School started tomorrow and the days would be folded into a tighter pattern, when it was all going to be harder, seeing Gabriel and roaming more or less as they pleased about the farm and into the secret part of the wood, planning the adventure, perhaps flying at last; Ruby's breath tightened when she thought about that. But all of it would be harder and, as the autumn drew on, and the evenings darkened – the first warning shots of winter – then the story they had been weaving together would, she just knew, drift further away and become more like a fairy tale.

Best of all, tonight, though, she wasn't scared, well, not really. There was nearly a full moon and this lane and the Mound was so much their place, hers and Peter's, it was as if her feet could find their way with no effort on her part. Perhaps, she thought, this was like flying, because already, here she was at the top of the Mound without quite realising how she'd got there. Leaning against the friendly trunk of the oak, Ruby looked towards the sea and saw the thin silver finger-lick of water marking the spot where land stopped and sky began. She shivered, but not with fear. Would Gabriel help her to fly from here to there, she wondered? It seemed so close and the farm was a painting in dark blue and shiny grey, where the moonlight glinted on the tops of trees and the white cowls of the oast shone like the towers in Sleeping Beauty's castle.

Ruby tried to pretend she'd stay only for a little while, that it was because she'd been at home all afternoon with Mum and Mina and all that sad talk about the War and people dying. Then when Peter had come back and there'd hardly been any time for him to tell her what had happened with Gabriel and everything because his mum had come and collared him to help lay the table for tea, she'd decided. It wasn't that she expected to run in to Gabriel, but she liked the idea that she'd be here and later he might too, in the caves at least. Maybe, if she was really brave, before she went home, she would just peer down there, because you never knew.

The churchyard

Peter and Ruby dragged behind the usual gang from the Leas on their way home from school. Back two days now and the weather still as hot as it had been all summer, hotter, it felt, stuck in school clothes again.

"So?" Peter scuffed at the dry grass lining the narrow track that led by the side of the graveyard. One of the oldest tracks in England, if not the world, someone at school had told him once, but he couldn't remember who. He wondered about ghosts as his foot struck a sharp piece of flint, all those people who must have walked here just as they were walking now. It was a thought that made him shiver.

"So, what?" Ruby turned round, heaving her satchel back on to her shoulder, casting a longing look at the ancient fat yew tree, which she'd wanted to climb, like she'd always done before the holidays, before – everything – but Peter wouldn't let her; said he'd tell and he meant it, she knew

"What were you doing at the caves anyway?" It was the first chance she'd had to talk to him properly since the other night. Every time she'd tried, either someone had appeared, or she couldn't seem to find the words. Privately, she knew he'd be upset. They did most things like this together and there she was creeping off in the middle of the night without even telling him. He wouldn't like it; and he didn't.

"What happened?" He sighed and glared at her. Just because she hadn't been able to go and see Gabriel with him and Oby, that's what it was about, he was sure of it.

"Nothing," Ruby admitted, shrugging, because mostly it was true; nothing had happened and Gabriel, who she'd gone there half hoping to see, hadn't turned up. Except –

"Ruby." He was going to get cross in a minute.

"Someone was there."

"What d'you mean? Gabriel? He came?" It had been arranged,

hadn't it, in any case? He'd go down and fetch the bits of canvas he needed.

"No, not him." Ruby frowned. "That's the thing, though, it wasn't him, well – oh I don't know."

"I don't get it," Peter grumbled, "first you're saying it wasn't him then – well, Rubes, what are you on about?"

Ruby tried again to get the picture in her head, because since that night she just hadn't been sure. She'd gone down to the entrance to the caves, the one where the stuff was being stored, not just because she hoped Gabriel might be there, but because she wanted to get close to that big secret again; it was like it was partly hers. But as she got to the entrance, meaning only to stand there for a minute before going home, because it was so dark and the silence of the black night had started to press down harder away from the open top of the Mound, as she stood there she heard the sound of breathing softly close by. Gabriel? Yet, something stopped her from calling out. If it was him, she reasoned, well, he'd step up to her and speak, they could have the talk she'd been imagining ever since she'd decided to come here. Ruby remembered how loud the beating of her heart felt, like a drum leading anyone to where she stood. And then?

"Ruby?" A hard grip on her shoulders, shaking her.

"I don't know," she said, it almost came out in a sob. She suddenly plonked herself down on the old milestone that lurked in the tall grass near the bottom of the track.

"What is it?" Peter was worried now. Had something horrible happened to Ruby that night? If it had it was most likely his fault, wasn't he supposed to keep on an eye on her? It was how it had always worked between them, until lately. Yes, lately everything had shifted; there was Gabriel, Oby. It wasn't like it used to be, just the two of them monging about the farm and the woods, making their games just for them, keeping away from grown-ups who mostly seemed too tired or too busy anyway. It had worked all right.

Now look.

Peter knelt next to her. "Tell me."

"I wanted to run away, but I was scared, case he followed and grabbed me."

"Who followed?" Was it Oby messing about, he wondered. Didn't seem like the sort of thing Oby would do, though. He wasn't a joker, not like Ruby who did like to catch people out, have them on. She wasn't doing that now, he was sure of it.

She stared at him. "I don't know! But it might have been the ghost, mightn't it?" She wanted him to say No, don't be daft.

"Well." It was true, since Gabriel, the Ghost Man seemed to have been forgotten about, mostly because they thought it was Gabriel that everyone had, for all those years, been calling by that name.

"See, I did hear, when I was running back along the path to the Lane, I did hear the funny voice that I've heard before."

"You never said anything about it." He stared at her.

"Didn't I?" Ruby thought, maybe she hadn't because it hadn't seemed important, but the voice spoke with strange sounds and it often sounded upset. How did she know that? It was like a dream that she'd had a long time ago, that suddenly broke back into her memory. It had been near the time when she'd had her accident and fallen out of the tree. After that, somehow, but she couldn't quite hold on to it yet.

"And he was cross, the man – the Ghost Man," she breathed the last words out on a whisper.

"What about?" Peter was puzzled. How come Ruby had never said before? See, that was another thing that had changed and got muddled between them. He sighed for the time before, when the only interruption to their life had been when hop-picking and all those Londoners arrived for the last part of the holidays. But it had just been part of the pattern, until this summer.

"Come on," he said finally, "we got to go, otherwise we'll get into trouble. You can tell me while we walk. All right?"

But Ruby didn't have much more to tell. She'd heard the breathing man, she was certain it was a man, and she'd smelt smoke, same as her dad. Then there'd been the voice upset and cross, making her even more afraid, so she'd run all the way home and slipped back in to the house and upstairs as quiet as she could.

In the wood

Was this mad? Gabriel stood staring at the pieces of canvas he'd cut. How could it be, he'd asked himself many times now, since the children had come up with the plan, well, since Oby had first mentioned it (what irony there!) – the very notion that he could rebuild the plane, that it could ever work and he'd find his way home.

"Home," he tried the word to see how it felt. Alien, that's how. He tried again, this time in the language of this place. "Home." Now it felt right. Home, home, home. If it was anywhere, surely it was here. In this wood, his cabin, furnished simply, a resting place in the woods, hadn't he dreamt of such a one when he was a boy? He and Herbert, God they'd camped out often enough together, slept under sky, star smashed and huge out there in the forest clearings. If he was nostalgic for anything it was that time, now lost in a much bigger and more haunting darkness than night could ever bring.

"It's another one of your games, Gabriel."

"Ah, I wondered where you'd got to." He felt almost relieved.

"Those children make you one of them. Is this what you have become now, a man turned child's plaything? Pah!"

"Dreaming is good, you were the one who always said so. Remember?" Gabriel turned, but didn't truly expect to see anything in this bright morning light. Night was the moment for such visions, when the world retreated into its softer shadowlands.

"You expect to see me!" So much anger now.

"No." Gabriel dropped his voice, and turned back towards the plane, beginning to lift the canvas, ready for trying its fit to the first hole. How strange, he had never noticed before, this was where the insignia had been and now look. It was split in half, damaged and broken, hardly recognisable as a cross at all.

"I am sad for you, old friend." The voice came again and did, indeed, sound sad. Gabriel was touched for a brief minute. Could this be the last visit and with it a kind of blessing? Forgiveness, even. He dashed that thought away. Nothing could forgive, nothing. Ever.

And if he got home, to that other home, he would most certainly be followed.

"My God!" Gabriel looked at his hands, holding them up and turning them over in the sunlight that was scattering through the tree tops.

"Red," came the voice, faint yet almost a growl.

"Red," repeated Gabriel, pushing his knuckles into eyes to stop the tears.

The oast house

Ruby parked her bike under the verandah where the fat hop pokes were stored until it was time to take them in and spread the newly-picked hops across the kiln floor ready for drying. It was so familiar to Ruby as to be almost unnoticeable. It was dark inside the oast, a sifted dark that held the warm, comforting smell of drying hops, making Ruby feel, as she always did, a little sleepy, sleepy and safe. Here her dad was King. She carried the warm pie dish carefully, nudging open the door to the bunk room and putting it down in the middle of the table, next to the always open can of condensed milk, there for the men's tea. Being Saturday night, her dad was the only one there. The other men went home at weekends to have a break with their families.

And tomorrow, Sunday, even her dad would be home for tea. It was his one day off a week, during hop picking. But tonight he ate here, alone, except if Ruby was allowed to linger and keep him company, if he wasn't too busy with the oast. Otherwise he scooped down his food quick, hardly noticing, sometimes, what it was he was eating, the careful thought that Ruby's mum put into making sure he had some decent grub inside him. It wasn't that he didn't appreciate it, just that his mind was on temperatures, drying, safety. Once, two years ago, there'd been a fire and since that he'd never been able to properly settle and have faith that he was in control. His face was creased with the worry of it, even when he was joking with the lads. It was like a scar that would never disappear.

She pulled her library book from her bag; maybe while she waited for him to come down from upstairs, she'd have a chance for a read in peace. Ruby yawned, first, she might have what Dad called forty winks, she was really very tired all of a sudden. Earlier, that afternoon, she and Peter had gone up to the wood, wanting to collect Oby and then go off to Gabriel's hut. When they didn't find him, the three of them trailed slowly through the trees to where the plane was, sure that he'd be there. He wasn't. What they did see was a pile of cut canvas left, rather carelessly, they decided, just dumped on the ground for anyone to see. Not that people generally came this far over, but still, what with the hoppers about and all, you couldn't be too careful, that's what Peter said as they'd gathered it up and pulled it inside the plane, out of sight. But as Oby rightly said, the plane was likely to be more interesting than any odd bits of canvas. No one was going to guess what was planned, were they? And, what's more, Peter had pronounced, if the London kids were going to find this place, or anyone else for that matter, then they'd have definitely done it by now.

It was a kind of comfort.

Maybe, Ruby had said, Gabriel would be at his cabin when they went back; but he wasn't and it seemed very empty somehow, as if he hadn't been there for a while. "Might be at the caves," Peter had said, but none of them suggested going there and since that night, Ruby was more than a bit afraid of the place, when she never had been before. It was a nuisance.

Instead they drifted back, Oby to the camp and the other two home to the cottages. Peter hadn't wanted to come down to the oast with her, so she'd got her bike out, feeling safer on that, though she couldn't have explained why, exactly.

Now in the quiet and peace of the oast, it all seemed far off and less worrying. Ruby could hear her dad above, walking about, sweeping the floors, ready for Monday's work. She climbed onto his bunk, opened her book, rolled over to the wall and straight away fell asleep.

She woke because there was someone else there, someone who wasn't Dad. There'd been a sound, what was it? A spoon, that was it, a spoon had fallen on to the brick floor, tinkling like a wake-up bell. The breathing, there it was; Ruby couldn't decide as she held her own breath in and listened, she couldn't fathom whether it was the same as the breathing near the caves, or not. If it was and she opened her eyes, then she'd know. That's daft, she heard Peter scoffing in her head, you'll only know who it is who's here now, silly!

"Gabriel!" Her voice sounded loud in the hummed silence.

"Shush!" He had his finger to his lips.

"Dad," Ruby slurred, her tongue still furred by sleep. "He's –"

"I know," said Gabriel, "I am here for my hops only, that is all."

Ruby swung off the bunk. "I don't get it." She rubbed her eyes, more sleep would have been good.

"Every year, I come for some of your father's hops, a small sample of hops he has dried, it is a reminder for me."

"What?" It was times like this that Ruby heard the strangeness in Gabriel's way of talking, he might have been someone from a story, or a play, but not an everyday person on the farm like the rest of them. It was what made him so special. A special friend, Ruby decided and someone who needed help, maybe, because a lot of the time he did seem to be upset and sad about something or other, as if he was trying to work out a problem that could never be worked out.

"When I was young," he was saying, but mostly to himself really, "I went hop-picking, and once I helped with the drying process too, it was a big honour for me. Long ago, now, long ago."

"What – here?" Ruby was confused.

Gabriel looked down at her, his sad half-smile not quite reaching his eyes, "No, little one, not here. Far away. Far away."

"Oh," said Ruby, only able to imagine a place like her own. The rambling oast, the familiar musty warmth of it, the martins nesting in the eaves year after year, the huge stacks of hop pockets steadily building in the store room at the far end as hoppin' drew on, the verandah where she practised her flying, always hoping – and outside the world of the farm, the woods, the orchards, the fields. All hers.

And now, since Gabriel, it had grown a little, as if the edges were less sharp than they used to be and the idea of elsewhere, out there and bigger and unknown, was something to wonder about, perhaps to explore.

Ruby shivered. "You are cold?" Gabriel asked, touching her lightly on the shoulder, the way her dad might.

"No," she said, swinging off the bunk and standing up, stretching, yawning a little. She eyed him cautiously. "You better be careful, though. Dad's funny about strangers in here and – "There was something else too, but she couldn't find the words, something about Gabriel and who – or what – he was. Didn't he, after all, belong to them, the children? The grown-ups had to be kept out of it. He was theirs, a secret, part of their game and not for sharing.

"Thank you, yes, I shall be. All I must do is collect my hops and then I shall go." He sighed and turned, but not before casting a weary, regretful look around the bunk room and at its simple comforts that spoke of homes nearby.

"I'll help, if you like." She opened her eyes wide at him.

"I – " He had been going to say No, but then decided that she needed him to say Yes.

"There are back stairs," she said.

He smiled and followed, of course he knew, but let her show him the way.

Charlie Moon took samples for the farmer and for other people and there were already a small stash of them, wrapped neat and square in their blue paper, up on the top floor, above where the hop pocket store was. Ruby sat on an old apple box and watched as Gabriel pulled one from the pile, turning it over in his hands as if it might be gold or other, more fragile, treasure.

"Does your father ever notice, I wonder," he frowned.

Ruby shrugged. "Don't know." She scraped her sandal along the dusty floor, making patterns, trying to write a G.

"Well," said Gabriel, bending to peer out into the evening. "I must go now."

"All right," she said and followed him down the stairs.

"Ruby?" Her dad was calling, he must have gone into the bunk room and seen his supper, seen her bike, most probably, but then she often wandered about, off and away, he called it, acting out some story that was stirring in her head.

Gabriel ducked under the stairwell, crouching low and fast into the triangle of shadow there.

"Dad?" Ruby called, uncertainly, glancing back at where Gabriel was hidden.

"Go to your father, quickly." The hiss came at her from the darkness and she ran on, sure that her dad would know exactly what she'd been up to and then what?

"Sorry, love." He looked at her, smiling, already starting on the pie, which was still warm, wrapped as it had been in one of her mum's pudding cloths and tied tight. "Forgot the time." His pocket watch lay on the table. "Watch stopped." He picked it up and shook it, nodding as it started its slow tick again. "Hop dust, I expect! What you been up to?"

"Nothing."

"Mooching, eh?" He smiled, slicing off more pie and offering her a piece, she nearly always had some, tasting as it did, so much better than anything on her own plate. "I've got the kettle on, make us some tea, eh? If you can manage all right?" He nodded at her arm, now out of its plaster and looking thinner and paler than the other sun-browned one.

"Course," she said, taking the big tin kettle across to the sink. It made her irritable, the way everyone thought she couldn't manage the simplest jobs since the accident, let alone get back to some real climbing again.

Afterwards, he came outside to see her off, watch her wobble back up the track to the cottages, like he always did, another ritual of hop-picking. She'd been hoping he'd go back inside and give her time to head off round the back where there was another, not much used door to the room where Gabriel was hiding, if he was still there. Ruby wanted to know he was safe, that he wouldn't be found by her dad. It was amazing that he never had been, if he did this every year. Every year and she'd never known, it sent a shiver of thrill down her back. At the top of the farmyard, where the gate was, she turned and looked back. Her dad had gone in now and she could see a light on upstairs in the oast, he must be up there checking the hops. She wheeled her bike round and set off back.

The door was slightly wedged open and she peered inside, calling his name softly. There was no answer and her voice seemed to fall dead and flat into the heavy dark. "Gabriel?" Ruby tried again.

"Forgot something, have we?"

She swung round and there was Stan, leaning against the broken bit of wall that would have once formed part of yet another roundel in this oast house, but now there were just the two, plenty, her dad reckoned.

"Peter," she stuttered the first thing that dropped into her head.

"Peter," Stan repeated, spitting a strand of tobacco into the hedge. "Hide and seek, then?" He was smirking, and there was that usual smell on his breath.

"Kind of." Ruby gripped her handlebars, wondering if she should just ride off as fast as possible. It felt safer, but something held her back; maybe it was that look in Stan's eye, telling her that he knew more than he was saying and that if she wanted to find out – well – then she'd better hang around and see.

"'Spect he's gone, though," she said.

"P'raps we should just check, though, eh? Make sure no one does any damage round here, what with your dad being in charge and all." Stan moved to the door and put his shoulder against it and gave a shove. He jerked his head for Ruby to follow him in and she was stuck now, if she didn't go after him he'd know she was lying. Although that might not really matter, it felt important to her to keep up this pretence with the touch wood hope that he wouldn't guess about Gabriel, or, even worse, find him if he was still in there somewhere.

"Hello!" Stan bent down, swaying a bit, Ruby wished she could push his bum so he'd fall on his stupid nose, making her waste time like this, when all she'd wanted to do was to pedal as fast as she could along the track to the wood to see if she could catch up with Gabriel before he got to the bridge, that being as far as she reckoned she ought to go at this time of day to be able to get home before it got really dark. "Well, well, very interesting." He was staring at a piece of paper, holding in the doorway and reading it in the fading pink sunset light.

"Most probably something Peter dropped," Ruby said, clenching her fists.

Stan turned to look at her, smiling in an unfriendly way. "If it is then he's a clever lad, very clever. Hiding his light under a bushel I'd say, if I was asked, that is."

Ruby didn't know what he was on about, but she tried to make it sound as if she did. "Well, he is," she said, "he knows loads more than me, about maths and everything." She had managed to see that there were numbers on the paper, what she hadn't seen was the writing, the notes that Gabriel had made for fitting pieces of the canvas to the plane.

"So," Stan looked about, peering back into the dark room, now solid with shadows, "nothing else." He sniffed like he was disappointed. "No one else, at any rate, eh?" He stared at her, waiting for her to answer.

"Dad," she said, daring him to ask more of his daft questions, "there's my dad, just upstairs. Shall I fetch him?" Ruby tried to move past him to get to the door that led into the main part of the oast, but he stretched out his arm across the entrance blocking her way.

"No, don't worry," Stan said, smiling again and this time making her shiver ever so slightly, "you leave that to me."

What did he mean? Ruby gaped at him. "I'd better get going," she said, "Mum'll be wondering."

"Yes," he said, not dropping his stare, or his arm from the doorway, "you'd better." He pulled a dog-end from behind his ear and cupped his hands together as he re-lit it. The smell, like when her dad was smoking, like that night near the caves. And the voice and, she realised now, what she'd heard was someone crying. Ruby frowned, trying to picture tears on Stan's face. Then ducked past before he had time to stop her.

Once she was outside, Ruby started to breathe properly again. It was too late to go after Gabriel now, he'd most likely be nearly back at his hut by this time, she hoped so. Stan gave her the creeps, it was like he could see right into her head and pick over her thoughts, pulling out her secrets.

It was just as she was cycling past the pigs that a whole gang of London kids tumbled out from the bushes, streaming after her, arms splayed out making that horrible noise that Mum said was the sound of the doodlebug bombs that whined overhead during the War, dropping without warning, a sound that they'd most likely learnt from their parents, who'd lived through it all, or not, some of them.

The caves

Next day, Peter called for Ruby and said that they should go to the caves because Oby had sent a message to say to meet there.

"How, sent a message?" Ruby asked.

"His aunty came to see your mum, didn't she?"

Ruby had forgotten, but yes, that was right. They'd gone off across Roman Fields together, walking to church; to remember, they said. When Ruby had said, Remember what? Her mum had pulled a sad face and told her not What, but Who.

"Is Gabriel coming too?" Ruby asked, as they pushed through the gap in the hedge. It was another warm day, although the sky was stranded with long lines of white, slashed through the blue, as if thousands of planes had passed that way.

"Don't know." Peter was bending down, pulling at something. "Ah, look!" he showed her. It was another fossil, a Shepherd's Crown, a piece of flint pressed with the image of a starfish dead now for a million years, or more. "You can have it if you like," he said, wiping it clean of earth before handing it to her.

"Thanks." She slipped it into her pocket. He'd given her lots before; maybe, she thought, when Peter wasn't looking, she'd give this one to Gabriel. Since finding the book in the library, she'd felt a bit left out of it all because the boys were the ones who were really helping. Oby had found the canvas, or his uncle had, and him and Peter had been a few times now, up to the wood to meet Gabriel and muck about with cutting it and working out how to fix pieces to the plane, talking about engines and how it might fly again. It seemed such a dream at times.

"So, what happened next?" Peter asked. Ruby had been telling him about the day before in the oast, with Gabriel and then Stan looming up like he did. She'd feel better if she could see

Gabriel, just to make sure he'd got back all right. If he hadn't it would be her fault, she knew it.

"He told me I could go."

"The paper," Peter was saying, "you said, he found this bit of paper with numbers on and you said it was mine and he said I was clever, or something?"

"I didn't get it," Ruby shook her head. "He's a bit do-lally that Stan, if you ask me."

"Most likely," Peter agreed; all the same, there was something wrong, but he couldn't put his finger on what, exactly. "Oh, well," he shrugged and peered again at the ground. There might be more fossils, something really rare, you never knew.

Oby was already inside the cave, pulling at bits of canvas and muttering to himself. Ruby waved the torch about, seeing how it threw up spiked, witch-hat shadows into the darker corners that led further back; you couldn't get to it, though, because the cave suddenly dropped back down into a tunnel again, getting narrower and narrower as it dipped downwards. They'd once tried throwing a rope with a weight on the end to see how far and how steep it went, and at first it fell gradually, then abruptly plunged down. It made Ruby shudder just to remember it, the thought of the pit, bottomless, maybe, not far from where they came all the time.

"Ruby!" Oby jerked his head. "Here, shine it here."

"What's up?" Peter climbed over a pile of chalk and looked. The canvas had been hidden as best it could be by some fallen chalk rubble, so that if anyone had put their head in, they most probably wouldn't take much notice, thinking it was rubbish, that was all.

"Dunno." But Oby was scratching his head and there was a smear of chalk dust on his nose. "It's just, it's just I thought there was more, loads more."

"Gabriel," Peter said, "expect he's taken it, He said he was going to be coming at night and getting bits, didn't he?"

"Maybe," Oby said, but he didn't sound very sure.

"The hoppers, p'rhaps?" Ruby liked to blame those kids, they were always teasing her, shouting names, jumping out from bushes and saying things about her. It was like they took over all the places that were theirs the rest of the year, took over without knowing what to do once they were there, hollering through the woods, beating at everything with their sharp, cut down sticks, peeing where they felt like it. Little buggers, her dad said. They didn't even go to school during picking, it wasn't fair.

"Come on," Peter said, after the three of them had stood there in silence, with only the sound of disturbed chalk, re-shuffling itself around them.

"Come on, what?" Ruby asked.

"We're supposed to be sorting out a sheet to take up to Gabriel. Aren't we?" He stared at Oby, who was still frowning and off somewhere else in his head, Ruby could tell even in this shadowed place. Mina said he was a worrier, and it was true, when you thought about it, his forehead was cracked by a crease almost all the time, had been ever since she'd first known him in Infants.

"Can I come?" Ruby felt she had to ask, because it had been boys, boys and she wasn't sure she was wanted.

"Course, don't be daft," Peter said. "Here, pull on this."

And together the three of them pulled a piece that would be manageable to carry between them and dragged it out to the cave entrance, where it lay in a crumpled heap, less exciting now it was in the glare of the polished sunlight. Oby had bought his bodge, but it was going to be difficult to get the canvas to fit, they could see that now.

"We'll have to cut it," Peter said, pulling his penknife from his trouser pocket.

"With that?" Oby didn't generally scoff.

"It'll have to do," Peter told him and bent down.

Oby caught his arm. "We don't know what size, though."

"Can't you just fold it smaller?" Ruby was eyeing up the horse chestnut by the stile, it had been a while since she'd had a good climb, what with her arm and everything. Suddenly she wanted to be up there, feeling the solid roughness of tree branches under her feet, sitting astride and staring down – unseen. The two boys were staring at her. Maybe when they got to the wood, while they were fiddling with the plane. Yes, that was it, she'd find a tree and have a good old go. It gave her a warm feeling.

"Look," she said, bending down and pulling at the sheet's corners flopped too big over the bodge's sides, so the wheels would never be able to turn. She took it off and held it like she'd done a hundred times when she helped her mum fold sheets, "Here." She gave them a corner each.

"Good on yer, Rubes," Peter whispered as they trundled down the track. Ruby smiled, satisfied. She could be a help after all.

"We should go the long way," Oby told them, "up through Spindles' Wood."

It was true, they could hardly go through the farmyard, even though it was Sunday; there were still people about and the hoppers' shop (really just a store off the tractor sheds) would most likely be opening soon and the place would be packed with Londoners chatting nineteen to the dozen and taking too much interest in the doings of anyone else on the farm.

They really mustn't be seen, not with this, especially not by Stan, they were all thinking, although none of them actually said his name. He lurked about them far too much. He was always asking questions and popping up where he wasn't wanted. She shivered when she thought about him and the sharpness that was always there too, didn't matter what his mouth was doing, his eyes stayed the same, small hard pebbles, dull and lightless.

In the wood

It was always the same after the children had left him; the hollow sense that it might be the last time he'd see them, that they were his anchor to the world and maybe even the rest of humanity. He smiled as he remembered them toiling towards him with the canvas. It was a touching sight and another for him to store and take out when the darkness almost threatened to overtake him. When he questioned them, he worked out that it must have taken them an hour, when normally it would be less than half that time. Just so that they would not risk being seen, all for him, that his secret would be kept safe. How could he have ever thought that he might not trust them? And how they had filled the terrible space left after the death of the bird, as if he couldn't be allowed too many good things in his life, he reflected. Yes, perhaps it was no less than he deserved.

He had come in here, inside the hollow tree, just to sit and smoke and cast a look over the plane. The plane! It was a lunatic adventure, but one that he could share so easily with them, caught as always when they appeared, by the simple magic of their belief in it all. And his promise to Ruby; it bothered him that he might not be able to honour it. The child was a real climber; the way she had raced up that pine earlier, like a forest sprite, sitting astride a high branch, calling out to them below about what she could see and young Peter squinting up at her, worried that she might jump and injure herself again. Gabriel had put a hand to his shoulder and Peter had smiled.

"She will be all right," he had tried to reassure the boy, "once, is surely enough." He cranked his arm into the crooked shape that Ruby's had been for those weeks during the summer and pulled a face of pretend pain.

Peter had laughed, "You look just like her!" He knew a good mimic when he saw one.

Gabriel laughed too, he had always been clever at mimicking others and he and his sister had often performed plays to the family in that long-ago other nearly forgotten time in that nearly forgotten place he had called home. All he had known and loved and wanted, until the slow beat of War had begun to stir, at first fracturing and then shattering the seemingly unalterable patterns of so many lives.

He thought of Herbert.

"My friend." His whisper brushed the still afternoon air now suddenly ragged with memories.

"Yes?"

"Remember those days?"

"Ah, days." Darkness spilled from the sigh that breathed so close, now, to Gabriel's ear.

"You were a climber too, eh?" Gabriel nodded to himself, recalling Herbert's agility, at first, when they were young, up the sides of houses, barns, even the school gymnasium once (that had caused great troubles for both of them, since Gabriel was the one on the ground, holding the stopwatch; Herbert was intent on breaking his own record for reaching the roof). Mountains were a later excitement and then Gabriel had climbed too; although reluctantly at first, he soon began to relish the peaceful clarity and space that higher altitudes had offered. Perhaps, in the end, it was what had tempted both of them into flying and then –

"A climber," the voice echoed.

"You saved my life," Gabriel said, drawing on his pipe and gone far back now to that moment, when his grip had found a loose hold and he had hung for a terrifying space believing that this would be the moment when his life would be snatched and thinking how he was too young, how there was so much still left to do in the world. If only he had known. Fortunately, for the both of them it was a future still unmapped.

"I saved your life." The voice was empty of emotion. Was there really no trace of irony there?

"I never thanked you properly."

"Such things are unnecessary and often without meaning. Don't you agree?"

Gabriel wiped his eyes and was silent.

"Don't you agree?" So much anger. He leant forward and pushed his head through the gap, peering into the soft gloom under the trees, hearing the shuffle of what sounded like foot-steps from the direction the children had left an hour since. Perhaps one of them was returning. He hoped not, for the sky was already draining into streaks of lilac; it would be dark before they had a chance to get home and he didn't much relish the idea of them being here too late in the day. Apart from others who might lurk here especially at this time of year, the wells were a distinct and real danger. He was always reminding them and often wanting to walk with them back to within sight of the camp, but they were so insistent that they knew the paths and he now and then caught the glances that slid between the three of them that spoke of another anxiety. He had to trust them in so many ways, surely this was just one more and it seemed unfair to burden them further. Even the thought, snagged half-formed in the back of his mind, put them into danger.

Hadn't he done enough harm?

A blackbird crashed among the bushes, twittering its alarm call. Gabriel eased himself from his hiding place, forgetting for a moment the shuffle of steps. It was as he stepped towards the plane, meaning to fetch the parachute to take back to his cabin to check for damage, that the figure moved quickly towards him.

"Gabriel," she said.

The farm

Ruby's dad hadn't yet left for the oast. Sunday was his day at home, but he still had to go and sleep there, ready to get the burners on for the next day. Picking would be starting early as usual, and the oast must be prepared. The other men got an extra night at home with their families, sometimes Ruby thought this wasn't fair, but Mum said that's what being Dryer and Manager meant.

"Like a king, then?" Ruby had once asked.

"Yes," her mum had smiled, "in a way."

And so the title had stuck and Ruby would bow to her dad on Sunday nights sometimes, after he'd given her a goodnight kiss, and call him Your Majesty. The year before she'd made him a crown, but it had got lost; she thought she would make him another one, better, made from hops and held together by some of the gold ribbon from the Christmas decoration box. Yes, she would. She was in bed, reading her book when the idea came and she decided to go up to the attic and find the box, so she could make a start on the crown tomorrow, as a surprise for Dad next time she went to the oast. She'd find a bine thick with hops tomorrow, when she got home from school and make it for him. She'd leave it on his bunk, yes, that's what she'd do.

Out on the landing Ruby could hear her mum and dad still talking downstairs, the door to the sitting room must have come open, Dad was always meaning to mend that latch. Ruby turned toward the attic stairs, she'd have to be quiet. Then she heard her name and stopped to listen; Dad was saying something about her. She risked going down one step.

"I don't like the way he looks at her, that's all."

"He's just a man full of sadness," her mum was saying, she always saw the best in people. "Broken up by the War, it happened to lots of them. And his dad running off with that young tart when he was just a lad. The bad way that girl treated him, the one he was engaged to. What was her name? Can't remember. All that, and the drink."

There was silence for a moment and Ruby wondered if that was all and she should just go up and fetch the ribbon, like she'd planned.

"And now this bloody piece of shit!" Sounded like paper being shaken, the way Dad sometimes did with the newspaper when he got cross about something. Pointing at the words, rattling the paper, angry because once things were written, they were hard to forget.

"You don't know it's him," Mum said shushing him.

"Put all me bloody hoppin' money on it. Wouldn't you? Eh, eh? Wouldn't you?"

"Yes," the word was mixed in with a sigh, "yes, I suppose I would. But maybe the best thing to do would be just to burn it, tear it up and burn it. Forget all about it. Eh, Charlie? Such a long time ago now. Why let it all boil up again, after all this while."

"Writing anonymous letters." He wasn't listening properly, Ruby could tell. "And that feather, all the feathers ever since – I don't know, sometimes I think I should have gone, carried me gun like the rest of them. Done me bit instead of sticking here." The armchair creaked as he slumped down into it.

"Listen. No, listen. You did the right thing. Somebody had to stay, keep the land working, keep us all fed. Eh? Eh? Come on love. I wish you wouldn't take it to heart so. It's all in the past. Over and done. Eh? Now then. Let me make another cup of tea before you go back down. Got some of that fruitcake left."

But her dad was still muttering. She wondered what it meant, guessing it must be something to do with Stan. What though? She sat down on the top stair and waited. Then she heard her dad get up and go out into the kitchen where Mum was putting the kettle on and fetching the cake tin from the larder. Unless she was willing to risk going further down, she most likely wouldn't hear much more. The letter, though. If only she could see it, find out what it said that was making her dad so angry – and not just angry. It was more than that. He sounded the way she did sometimes when things seemed so unfair she wanted to cry. It was just like that. And there was another thing. What had he meant about Stan looking at her? Ruby thought about it, trying to remember that last time when he'd caught her in the oast, the way his eyes were, cold as pebbles, like they were trying to fix her to the spot so she couldn't move until she'd told him what he wanted to know. The secrets that she and Peter and now Oby held close and tucked away out of sight of other people, especially blokes like him.

"Ruby, love? What's up?" She was so caught up in the whirl of thoughts that she hadn't noticed her mum come to the bottom of the stairs. "You not feeling well?"

"Thirsty," Ruby said and it wasn't quite a lie, now she thought about it her mouth did feel dry.

"Bit warm up there." Mum came up and felt her forehead. "Come on, back to bed and I'll fetch you a drink."

Ruby didn't move.

"Come on." Ruby got up and let herself be tucked back under the eiderdown, while Mum went downstairs. She seemed to be gone a long time and when she came back with a glass of water and a hot water bottle, she was frowning and sad.

"Mum?" Would she say? Ruby wondered, all that stuff about the letter.

"You just drink up and lie down now, like a good girl, eh? School tomorrow."

School. It was such a nuisance, having to go at the moment when there was so much to do with Gabriel in the wood, things to find to help him build his plane, a chance for her to climb more trees to keep lookout. It had been decided that could be her job while the others got on with cutting canvas and wood. But Gabriel had told them that they must go to school, that school was important where you learnt about the world and what had gone on in history so you could learn from it. Ruby wondered what they might learn from the Romans, because that's what they were doing in history at the moment. Peter liked it, though, and was always on the lookout for bits of pots or coins, especially as they walked home through Roman Fields. He reckoned that they'd made a big camp there after they'd invaded, and that the Mound was most likely a lookout too. It was one of their games when they couldn't think of anything else, or when real adventures, like this one, weren't happening.

"Invaded?" Ruby had asked Peter.

"The Roman army," he said, "they came over the Channel in their boats and took over."

"Like the War?" Ruby said.

"Kind of," Peter told her, then smiled, "except this time, we won."

"Oh." But it was all such a long time ago, Ruby thought, what did it matter now?

She felt sleepy and warm and the water had eased her throat. Then just as she was tipping over into sleep she thought she heard Mum come in again and whisper something about not worrying, it didn't mean anything and if she had her way she'd burn the bloody thing, but Charlie – she'd stopped then, realising she was thinking aloud, but Ruby knew what her mum was talking about and she was going to find a way of seeing that letter. And why would anyone write a letter to someone they saw nearly every day? It was a puzzle. She'd talk to Peter tomorrow.

In the wood

After she'd gone Gabriel returned to his cabin. At first he thought he should stay there, make a new camp in the hollow tree, because no one else knew about that and although once he had come very close to telling the children, he was glad that he had held his tongue. There must be some things they should not know, some things they could not. He shivered when he thought about it, held up his face to the sky as if there might be forgiveness there. Where else, now?

"Gabriel," she knew his name. But how had she known, unless one of them had told her, talked about him? It was so dangerous. He was no longer safe here. Perhaps his other plan, walking to the coast, getting across somehow, was the better, more realistic plan after all.

"Yes, I am Gabriel."

And she'd sat down on a long ago sawn and abandoned tree trunk, as if just hearing his voice was enough to unsteady her.

"Did – " He hesitated, even asking the question felt a little like a betrayal. How strange, because, wasn't he the one who had been betrayed, by Oby, he supposed looking at the woman. She was obviously from the camp. His mother? No, he didn't think so.

"Oby?" He stared at her, waiting for her to lift her head, she seemed to be examining her hands as if she'd just noticed them.

"No." She shook her head and now looked at him. Her eyes, in spite of her age, were bright, dark brown against the clear white, like the chocolate sweets he'd eaten as a boy. He'd completely forgotten about them until now, such a warm memory, Christmas time and sweets for all the children from the tree. Strange that this woman should spark it back for him, like a gift unbidden.

"One of the others?" This was half to himself.

"No, you misjudge them, they keep your secret as well as they can. I guessed, that's all."

"Guessed? But my name, how did you know my name?"

"I found a note that Oby had dropped, from Peter. Something about canvas and, well. I put two and two together, you see. The canvas came from the camp where I live, my Joe. Oby asked for some and Joe, well, he said yes, he never refuses the boy."

Gabriel could imagine that. Oby had a steady and quiet charm, that seemed to give him a special quality when it came to decisions, Gabriel had seen it when the other two were around. They trusted him to do the right thing and not to let them down, and, he now understood, he had the same regard for the boy.

"And then, today, I was up this way and thought I'd follow him. I was worried, that's all."

"Yes, yes," Gabriel was thinking. The way she looked at him after he had spoken, the change in her face. This was going to be difficult. He wished he had more time to consider what he should do for the best.

"See, Mister, I'm sure you'd feel the same, eh? If they were your young ones." She tucked a strand of her hair back into its looped braid. It had been so long since he'd seen a woman with hair dressed in this manner. That and her words gave him a sudden sharp twist of pain, homesickness and something worse. A lie revealed as a lie, perhaps.

"Mister?" She had stood up and was touching him lightly on the hand.

He roused himself. "You are right – " He swallowed the word before it formed in his mouth. Her name, that was it, he must ask her name.

"Mina," she said, bowing her head slightly to one side. He saw that she still held beauty in her face, beauty and strength. That and her warmth, for in spite of her coming to him like this, full of concern for the children which might almost be accusing, in spite of this he knew she was a fair person and someone who could be trusted. Or was that just his wishful hope?

"I mean them no harm." He held his palms to her and caught her stare as he did so.

"Oh." She backed away for a moment, her hand to her mouth.

"Mina," he said, moving to steady her in case she might fall, she seemed suddenly unsteady.

"Sorry," she muttered, "sorry." She shook her head now and gulped, "It's nothing, just – "

"You must believe me," he tried, wondering how to reassure her, "I would never harm children. Never."

"Really?" It might almost have been a sneer shadowing her face for a brief second, but then it was gone, the even calm restored and her nodding carefully, weighing his words as she had before.

"They have become – " He turned to look at the half buried plane, touchingly so much a part of their lives and expectations now. "Friends," he finished, smiling at her for the first time. "Truly. And I value and thank them for it. It means a great deal to me, alone as I am." He was surprised to feel tears welling, that he might cry in front of this woman, it was an odd notion, yet not without a certain appeal.

"You have a lot of sadness," she said, making it sound simple.

"Yes." There was no other answer.

"This," she nodded towards the plane now, "is this what they come for, a game, eh?"

"Game, yes, I suppose it is and – " He wanted to say how it had all happened at first by accident, because of Ruby's accident, falling out of the tree, otherwise he might never have got involved with them all, but that having become caught up with them he couldn't – wouldn't – change the pattern. Maybe he had been more than a little mad before. Still was, if he thought about it, after all there was Herbert and that surely spoke of imbalance at the very least. He stared at her.

"How long have you known about me, here?" He hadn't meant it to come out quite so harshly and once more she stepped back.

"The Ghost Man," she said, staring hard at him, "we have all talked of him."

"Me?"

"You, well, it must be mustn't it? Unless there is another." She looked at him strangely.

He was caught off guard for just long enough, "You have seen him?"

Again, she was looking at his hands, a cloud of fear crossed her face, he might have said, it was as if she knew.

"You have seen him," this time it wasn't a question.

"No," she said, shaking her head, "no, I haven't seen him."

"But you know how he follows me and comes to me?"

"Yes," she said, sad again, sad for him it was written in her eyes, a woman of compassion so obviously.

Afterwards, when she had gone, he wondered that why he hadn't asked her more, but had instead accepted her answers the way one, when dry with thirst, might a take a cup of clear water when offered. It had seemed as natural and as necessary as that. What he had asked was if there was any way he could stop it, this haunting, because that's what it was, of course. Odd that he'd never thought of it in those terms before, not until he'd heard her use the words Ghost Man. To all intents that was he, the one who moved by stealth and mostly under the cover of dark, to take the things he needed, no more. It was what the children had called him at first, among themselves, casting him wary looks, but this soon passed, and then he became just Gabriel.

Mina had stared at him for a long moment before answering his question that time, as if she was measuring his ability and strength to cope with the truth of what she must say.

"My experience of such things, tells me, Gabriel – " She hesitated and the way she spoke his name reminded him again of a past time, once in the forests near his home he had come upon a boy from a tribe such as hers, he guessed, who had also spoken in this fashion. His heart ached for the innocence of that lost part of his life.

"Please," he said, "continue."

"It tells me that you can never be free of it, such things stay with us for life – as they should," she muttered, not daring to look him in the eye in case she shouted her buried anger at him for all those other lost ones too.

"Yes." It was true and almost a comfort to hear it spoken by another. "Even if I go home, he will follow."

Mina nodded. "I should go," she said casting a look at the softening light, dusk was not far off and they might worry back at the camp; she had told her sister, Oby's mother, that she was going to search for some blackberries from her secret place. Mina was well known for such secrets and everyone respected them, knowing they would be tasting the fruit in one of her pies before too long anyway.

"You are – " Gabriel searched for the word, "satisfied?"

"Yes," she said, "I suppose I am."

And it was only after he was back in his cabin, drawing some comfort from one of his pipes, that he realised Mina's visit had not just been about the children, but something deeper and darker. He had sensed, he reflected, as the rest of the day's light drained into deeper pink and then to purple, that if she'd had a knife she might have finished him then and there; perhaps that would have been, after all, for the best.

The hop garden

It was what they often did after school during picking, wandered up to find their mums and help fill the last of the day's baskets. And that day a photographer was wandering the farm looking for some seasonal colour, taking pictures mostly of the Londoners who were always ready to pose and full of teasing and stories about the adventures they were having. Then he came down the alley where Peter and Ruby were and suddenly Ruby really wanted him to notice her. Didn't she look especially pretty in her faded pink and blue dress and her hair done in a single thick plait, shiny as a chestnut?

"Stop it," Peter muttered at her, knowing exactly what she was up to. He hated having his photo taken. But the bloke had already seen them and was fiddling with his camera, framing where they were standing under a swaying, toppled bine, look-ing, as it did, like a huge bunch of grapes in an old painting.

"You two!" he was calling.

"He wants to take your picture," Ruby's mum smiled, encour-aging them to look up, Ruby didn't need encouraging.

"Turn towards me, little girl. All right?"

"Like this?" Ruby could be flirty sometimes, Peter realised. It was the way she was with Gabriel too, though not always.

"Lovely," the photographer was saying, "lovely." And to Peter's relief he then took some of just Ruby. Afterwards he came up to them and started chatting, asking questions. About hop picking at first.

"Name's Bob. I'm not from these parts," he explained. But they could tell that as soon as he opened his mouth, "I'm a northern lad, me." He laughed as if it was funny. "What about you?" He was trying to be friendly, Peter knew, because he must have noticed how uncomfortable he'd been, having his photo taken.

"Here," said Peter, wishing he'd go; that camera made him uneasy.

"And you, young lady?" The bloke squatted in a chummy

way next to where Ruby was filling her basket with the big soft green hops.

"Here." Ruby was suddenly and unusually shy and had gone red, Peter saw.

"We live here," he told the photographer. So why don't you just bugger off and leave us alone? But he didn't say that.

"Those woods," the man said, standing up now and staring, "great stuff!" He stroked his chin for a moment and then started fiddling in his bag. "Slide film," he explained to Peter who didn't want to be, but was now just a bit curious. "Colour," the bloke went on, "the trees, wonderful colours. If I could get the hops and the wood and the sky – " He carried on staring and thinking aloud to himself.

"People live there," Ruby blurted, wanting him to notice her again.

Peter glared at her. What was she thinking of? He could see their mums listening now.

"Do they now?" His eyes were sharp and thoughtful. "And what kind of people would they be, then, eh?"

"Gypsies," Peter said, quickly, because that was true and then he straight away felt bad, next this bloke would be going to Oby's camp and trying to take their pictures too. They might not want that, mostly they weren't keen on strangers. Now look.

"And there's the Ghost Man too," his mum said, laughing, seeing that Peter was in a fix, hoping to put the man off maybe.

"Ghost Man?"

Peter clenched his fists and couldn't look at Ruby, but he'd heard her take a breath. "Just a stupid story," he said, "no such thing as ghosts in any case. Everybody knows that."

"Gypsies and a ghost," the photographer smiled at them, "and all them trees. I should go and take a look, maybe." He started to pack his camera away in his bag. "Where're the gypsies, did you say?"

"There are some just down the end of this alley," Ruby's mum said, coming to the rescue. It was true, Oby's mum was down there with some of the other women from Mina's camp, although neither Mina nor Oby were about. Perhaps they'd tell this bloke where to go, Peter thought and then he forget all about the wood, the gypsies and, most of all, the Ghost Man.

"I'd like to have a look up there, though." He wouldn't be put off. "The leaves, champion colours they are, remind me of up home."

"Beech," Peter said, who knew all about trees, "that's why. And there's another wood, down by Saxon Hop Garden, across there," he waved his hand towards the farm.

"And there's the oast too," Ruby's mum said, she could see the two of them were worried about something and she didn't like the way the bloke was pushing at them. Hadn't he got his photos? Surely that was enough.

"The oast?" That got him, he swivelled round to look at her.

"Where they dry the hops," Ruby said, "my dad's in charge."

"Is he?" He scratched his head. "Heck, I don't know where to start now." He threw a glance towards Oby's mum and the others, they weren't looking too friendly now he thought about it.

"He's the dryer."

"Would he mind, d'you think?" He wasn't sure which was Ruby's mum so he slid a look between them both.

"I'm sure he wouldn't," Ruby's mum told him. "Why don't you go and ask? They should be pressing around now."

"Pressing?" He screwed his face up.

"S'where they shovel the dried hops into pockets," Ruby explained.

"Sacks," Peter said. Anything to get this bloke away from here and away from the wood. "Big long sacks," he stretched his arms out.

"Well, that does sound amazing." Bob looked towards the wood and sighed, "guess anyone can take pictures of trees in the autumn, eh? But all this, it's like being abroad, I'm telling you!" Ruby's mum smiled and Peter almost cheered.

"Maybe Peter and Ruby could take you," she said, which wasn't quite what Peter had in mind, but if it meant the bloke stopped nosing about the wood and everything, perhaps it was best they do it.

"All right," he said, "come on Rubes."

"We'll show the bomb 'ole on the way," Ruby said, "if you like?"

Peter sighed, couldn't she keep anything to herself?

"And is the bomb still in there?" He was making fun, couldn't she see that?

"Oh, no, well, don't think so anyway." She looked at Peter.

"They found bits, remember?" No harm in talking about this, he supposed.

"Bits of the bomb?" The bloke looked surprised.

"Yeah, my dad's still got some," Ruby was showing off again, doing little twirls on her toes, hoping Bob might say something about how she ought to be a dancer, Peter knew that, because it's what she often asked people, ever since she'd been a fairy in the school play in Infants'. That was where all the flying stuff had come from too.

"Well, I'd like to see that," Bob said.

"Were you in the War?" Ruby squinted up at him.

He laughed a bit too loud. "I'm not that old – cheeky madam!"

"Oh." She wandered to the edge of the track and did a quick cartwheel on the grass.

"My old man was, though." Bob was stroking his chin again, his eyes gone a bit sad, staring off into the distance. Maybe he wasn't so bad after all, Peter thought, just because he took pictures and asked questions.

"Was he – did get shot at?" Peter knew his dad had been shot at and had, most likely, shot at some people back and he guessed it was the same for lots of dads, except Ruby's of course, who hadn't fought.

"Yes, and taken prisoner too, didn't come home 'til the end."

"Cor!" Ruby stared at him, as if he still carried with him some of that long ago adventure.

"Nasty business," said Peter, who'd seen what it had done to his dad and didn't much like fighting, although he'd punch back if he had to.

"You could say that, lad," Bob's face went shadowed and dark. "Bloody – " he glanced at them, "sorry kids. Makes me angry, that's all, seeing him like he is now, like a husk, like one of these, see?" He bent down and picked up the prickle case that had held a chestnut. "That's what war does, sucks you in, chews you up and then – " he spat, "if ever I got my hands on the bastards who – " He stopped then, remembering they were there, suddenly grinning and changing back to the larky bloke, teasing Ruby and making Peter feel out of it again.

And all the way to the farm Ruby was showing off, telling Bob about hop picking and treating the place like she owned it. Peter just followed on, kicking now and then at the bits of flint that stuck out of the dusty track.

The camp

Gabriel wasn't sure why he'd come, it was as if he'd wandered there half in a dream, perhaps that was it. Hadn't he been dreaming, hearing Herbert's voice again, telling him that he would never go home and that if he did, by some miracle, do so, then who would know him or want to know him? If they ever discovered what he had done, but, he sometimes argued with himself (or with Herbert, he could never be sure) – wasn't their crime just as great if not greater? One, a hundred, a thousand, a million. Eventually, you had to face it, Gabriel concluded, darkness was darkness, however it was measured.

It was nearly a week since he'd seen either the children or Mina, although he had been working on the plane, trying to show, when they did come, that he had made progress and that – yes – it would happen. It must happen.

And now, here he was in Friday's early dusk, lurking in the soft purple shadows on the edge of Oby's goat pen. How empty it seemed without Nancy! Oby's uncle had brought another goat, but Gabriel knew from Oby that it would never be the same;

Oby had bottle-reared Nancy as a tiny kid. Such a waste, cutting the animal's throat like that, rather like the waste of the death of his bird. Who would do such a pointless thing? If he believed in ghosts, Gabriel might have thought it was Herbert, who, after all, had reason enough to smear Gabriel's life and the lives he touched, with a kind of just revenge.

But he didn't.

"Why are you here?" Mina had come out from the pen.

Gabriel lifted his hands. Truly, he did not know, unless it was for this very moment, to see Mina again to try and grasp what it was he was doing and why.

"Do you have a knife?"

She stepped back in surprise.

"Please," he said, "do not be alarmed. It is just that I wondered if – " He stopped, seeing that she really was afraid, fearing that perhaps he had lost his mind, something he wondered often enough about himself, especially recently.

"I thought, you were the one." Her voice was low, more like someone humming a lullaby than someone speaking. Strange. For a brief moment it shifted Gabriel to his childhood and a memory of his mother (or was it his sister?) leaning over his cradle and singing him to sleep. Time snatched at him as he remembered the old, familiar song.

"The one?" He realised she hadn't finished.

"With the knife." She took a deep breath and held her palms open as if to show she meant no harm, although it was a strange business this. She, a tiny gypsy woman and this man, so tall and strong-looking, he might have been part of one the trees he walked amongst. A trunk or a branch, with the same earthy rightness and endurance. She was suddenly no longer afraid.

"I did not do it, madam." Except he didn't call her madam, but another word, that made her shiver slightly, as if with an echo from somewhere far away.

"No," she said, lowering her eyes now, "I am sorry for saying it. I know you didn't."

"Whoever it was," Gabriel went on, encouraged by the warm truth of her words, "also, I think, killed my hawk."

"Yes," she said, "I'm sure he did."

So, she knew! He wanted to ask, but dare not for some reason. Obviously, she had been testing him out too, or herself, maybe.

She sat down on an upturned apple box. "Why did you ask about the knife?"

"I – I am not sure. It was a silly question I think." He couldn't tell her the truth, for then she would believe him to be mad and perhaps would somehow make it impossible for the children to continue to see him. That notion was as painful as a blow might be.

"Do you need a knife?" Mina stared at him, frowning.

He shook his head, gesturing towards his pocket.

"Of course," she said and then her face caught in a sudden last burst of sunlight as it dipped below the canopy, smiled gently at him. "You must not think of such a wrong act, Mister. Life's a precious token, you know, a sweet and lovely thing." She nodded and he found that he was nodding back as if sealing a bargain.

"What are you doing here?" Mina asked after a moment's quiet.

Later, when it was truly dark and he was back sitting outside his cabin, drawing smoke through his clay pipe, Gabriel pondered on what had happened. It was, he half smiled to himself, as if he'd intended that all along; that he should go to the camp in an almost dreamlike way, find Mina and talk to her. The lifting of a great burden, that's what it had been. At last, to be able to tell another person. He glanced up as a blackbird crashed through the low branches of the young beech, they were such nervous birds, weren't they, often rattling out their alarm call and yet when they sang, so fluidly beautiful, like water in song, more than any human could every achieve – surely? And such innocence, too.

The way Mina had been, after he'd finished his story; for what seemed like a long while, she didn't speak, or even look at him. Instead she had examined her own hands, turning them over, first one and then the other and then pressing her thumb across the palm, as if to smooth away the creases there.

Finally: "He was your friend."

"Yes," he answered, although it hadn't been a question, "from boyhood, as I said."

"Many years, then?" She gave him a steady look that was hard to read.

"Oh," he had shrugged, "so many." But actually, how many? They had both been just twenty when the War had begun and had known one another since they were nine or ten, meeting after Gabriel's family had moved. So, now he had to consider it, he calculated that it really hadn't been that long at all. Less time in fact than –

"I can see you have death about you," she said, managing not to accuse him and yet he deserved it and more. "I knew it from the first."

"Well, you were right." There was no use denying it, not now, not after what he'd told her.

"And all those others too," her whisper had drifted across the space between them, the words not meant for him, but some private acknowledgement of her own.

He replied, nevertheless, "Yes, I am very sorry for it, for all of it." The words couldn't begin to cover what he meant, or the pictures that sprang to him (and to her, he guessed), but it was the best he could do.

"Why?" The whites of her eyes were moon-bright in the dying day's light.

"Why?" For a moment he thought she was asking too big a question: why all those others? Then he understood, she was asking about Herbert. That was all.

"As I said," he was struggling now, after it had been so easy before, "he wanted to go and I wanted to stay. We had an argument, it ended – "

"Badly?" Was she smiling? He couldn't tell.

"And – " He suddenly knew that there was more to it, something that had been growing in him over these past fifteen years. "We felt differently about things."

Mina would surely be raising her eyebrows at this, but he couldn't see her face clearly now. "Yes?" she said.

"He was – " Where was that word? "Committed," yes, that was it, "to it all. More of a believer."

"And you weren't?"

Gabriel remembered how it had been, or how he thought it had been. Herbert egging him on, saying what fun it would be, caught by the glamour that had been pulling at them, and so many of the young (and not so young) for years. A way to escape the boredom and depression of the hard times. War and such a war too – like a huge campaign from a richer and more glittering past, touching the raw emotion that was, maybe, in every knight and every knight's lady, that the flags massing and the riding off to fight were what gave soul to a people. All of this had caught Herbert and, by association and because they had shared more or less everything like brothers, it had captivated him too. And in war, there were bound to be winners and losers, the victors and the victims. It was the nature of the thing, the beast as Gabriel's mother had called it in an indiscreet moment in the local baker's, causing a shimmer of disapproval (or was that fear?) among the other customers.

"I don't know," was his answer.

"Honest?" She wasn't letting him off that lightly, then.

"Perhaps," he admitted. After all, it was true, when they had both joined the air force they had a lot of fun as young cadets, plenty of hard training, but hard playing too and excuse for parties whenever they were on leave, with plenty of girls ready and willing to be impressed – and more – by their uniforms and their cocky-rule-the-world manner. "But I wasn't a true believer," he said, firmer now.

"Yet it still all happened, eh, Mister? All that killing and those places, all that waste."

He felt his face heating and could only nod, speaking might bring tears. She was right and he was wrong. She was part of the winning side, wasn't she? Right, then, had won in the end. And those last moments when he and Herbert had fought, literally fist to fist for a while, Gabriel had shouted at him that he was a murderer, that they were all murderers and he wasn't prepared to do it any more. That was when Herbert had called him a coward and when he had, without thinking, on impulse pulled out his gun.

"Where is he buried?" Mina had asked, unexpectedly.

Gabriel told her and she said she would, if he didn't mind, take some of the last of the roses that grew down by the river near her camp. He was strangely touched by this thought, as if it was on his behalf and might start to heal the terrible wound that he had carried all these years.

"Please do," he said, "I should like that very much." And she had nodded, getting up to mark the end of their talk, but before she disappeared into the spreading dark, she called back to him – her last words.

"The children, you will be careful with them?"

The farm

It had been Peter's idea and no one had suspected, although Mum had given them a sideways look and even said something to Ruby early that morning.

"You gone off hoppin' love?"

"No, no, Mum." The words came out in a rush tangled together by guilt. Ruby felt as she always did when she lied, especially to Mum, as if her thoughts were there above her head, clear as daylight for anyone to read. "Peter and me, he's – "

"Doing some homework, yes, he said," Mum looked at her steadily, like she was giving her the chance to say what they were really up to. "Funny, though."

"What?" Ruby was diddling with the piano, wondering if she could remember how to play My Bonnie Lies Over the Ocean.

"You don't normally get this much homework, do you?" Ruby's mum started cramming sandwiches and apples into her bag; they usually ate in the hop field and even though it was Saturday and they finished earlier, she always packed some fuel in, as she called it.

"It's a special thing." Ruby pressed the fingers of her left hand hard on to one of the deep thunder notes.

"Oh," Mum said, "a special thing. I see."

"Yes," said Ruby, sliding off the piano stall and skipping off outside to look for Peter.

"There's a sandwich for you in the pantry," her mum shouted as she walked off down the back path, heading for the farmyard and the trailer where some of the pickers got a lift to the hop garden. Luckily, they'd finished the Bower for the moment and were at the other end of the farm near the main road, in Saxon Fields. It meant that there was less chance of her and Peter being seen when they went to Bower Wood to find Gabriel. And it was almost true, except the homework bit, because the plane and trying to help to begin to rebuild it was a kind of special thing that any teacher might think was useful. All that arithmetic, Peter had pointed out, when they were working out the plan on their way home from school the day before. And he was right, him and Oby and Gabriel had been scribbling lots of numbers down on bits of paper. Measure twice, cut once, Ruby's dad always said and it was something she had repeated to Gabriel, who had murmured them softly to himself, smiling and shaking his head and trying each word slowly, like he often did when they, but especially she, said things to him.

Ruby had thought it would be harder to have to explain why they didn't want to go picking on Saturday, they'd always, always done it forever and even when the year before Ruby was getting over chickenpox she'd gone, because it was hoppin' and a kind of magic time of year. Even the air smelt different, filled with rich, warm bitter smell of hops. And there were different sounds too, strange voices, laughter and singing, people and dogs where normally it was quiet and empty.

"Just say," Peter had told her. "It'll be all right, honest. But don't say too much," he warned, always Ruby's downfall and the way she was often caught out.

"See, told you," he said when he came round after his mum had gone off too. "It's the best time, Saturday, when they're all busy at the other end of the farm. We can get on in peace."

Then, just as they were about to go, Ruby remembered how Gabriel was always asking them to take him the old newspapers. Always, like they were food, the way he asked, his eyes sad and worried. There were plenty lying around, waiting to be used to light the fire and she pulled some from that pile, which was when she found it.

Peter was waiting outside, sitting, patient as usual on the back steps. He squinted up at her, she was out of breath suddenly, with nervous excitement. "What's up?"

They read together, neither of them speaking for a minute or so. Finally, Peter spoke. "It's the one you said about, this letter, then?"

Ruby nodded, "On the fire pile."

"Funny, though," Peter frowned, "you'd think he'd have chucked it on the fire straight away."

"P'raps he wanted to find out who it was from?"

They looked at it again, written in capital letters on cheap notepaper, torn with a ragged top edge, like whoever had written it couldn't be bothered, or didn't know how to care about such things.

Peter looked out down across the garden to the orchard at the bottom, where the leaves on the cherry trees were already starting to turn the faintest of gold and where the breeze was stirring among the branches like the beginning of a dance. "He most likely knows, though." His words whispered through the blue air, "most likely, Rubes."

"Stan," she said.

And Peter nodded, slowly. "Come on, we'd better get on."

"What shall I do with it?"

He stared at her. "Put it back, I reckon. It's your dad's letter."

She waited, not sure, wanting somehow to keep it, let Stan know they knew, make him say sorry for writing such nasty things. And not only nasty, rude too, "You were a fucking coward then and you're still one now." Ruby felt hot when she thought about it. Fancy writing it down like that! It was about the War, she knew, because the rest of the letter said something about fighting for your country and how some people had guts and some people didn't and never would. Her dad was funny about Stan, always had been, not letting him work in the oast, not ever really speaking to him even when the men were all in the Half Moon together, but her mum said Stan preferred drinking to talking, anyway. Now she thought it about she supposed that must be the reason. It didn't seem fair, though, her mum had always said that Stan had fought bravely, why should he be so horrible to her dad, who'd helped keep the country fed? That's what they'd learned at school, which was just as important a job as going out and shooting the enemy.

"I'd put it back, Ruby," Peter said, "we know what it says and most probably who wrote it. Better leave it. Come on." It didn't seem right to her, though, it was different for Peter, his dad had been in the army too, so it wasn't the same at all. Ruby wanted to do something to make Stan stop, to make him be a nicer man than he was; the letter might be a way of doing it, although she wasn't sure how, exactly.

"Ruby!" Peter was already at the front gate. He could be bossier than her when he put his mind to it.

She pulled the back door shut, locked it and ran after him.

The Mound

Gabriel knew it was risky being up here during the day and a Saturday too when there were more people around, but then at this time of year, there were always more people. All those pickers, their children and their visitors, talking in a manner that he still found hard to understand, although over the years he had started to unravel some of their words. He knew enough now to grasp that he must never been seen by any of them, he and his kind were still hated by so many and if they knew – well, savagery was not something that was ever likely to go away, not even after all that had happened, it was so easy to justify.

He would go back to his wood soon, the children might come and wonder where he was and he wanted to see them more than he could have imagined, as if there were an urgency. But what could that be? The plane, he supposed, yet it was something that was going to take a long time and the notion of getting it to fly was hardly feasible, when he allowed his mind to travel over all the mechanics of it. Yet, it was not impossible and the children's belief in it and in him pulled it within reach. A dream, a good dream and a kind of recompense for the past, at least in some small way.

Gabriel smiled and lifted his head into the breeze that was coming straight off the sea which gleamed thin and silver on the horizon, like a promise.

The camp

Ruby was holding a basket of blackberries, some picked by Oby and his sister and the rest from Mina, he told them, mostly to take to Gabriel, his aunt had said; she thought they could share them and maybe, next time she'd make a blackberry and apple pie. Aunt Mina had taken a liking to Gabriel and Ruby wasn't sure how she felt about it. Pleased, mostly, but Gabriel was supposed to be their special and secret friend: hers, Peter's and Oby's. It didn't seem quite right and made her uneasy, the other two weren't happy either, she could tell.

"Does she know about the plane, as well?" Ruby asked.

"Shush!" Peter glared at her, they were up by the now empty goat pen, but Oby's sister had been trying to tag along with them and even though he'd made her go and play with some of the little ones, she was still throwing looks in their direction.

"No," Oby said, although he didn't know. Surely, thought Ruby, Gabriel wouldn't tell her about that?

"That's all right, then." But Ruby was annoyed with him, as if it was his fault Aunt Mina had got involved. And she was more than annoyed, jealous too: Gabriel was hers, she had been the only girl in the gang, Mina, even though she was as old as Mum, had changed that now.

"Come on," Peter slid down from the gate, "we should get going, half the day'll be wasted else. And look." He nodded towards the fire, where Oby's sister, for once wasn't watching them.

In the wood

Gabriel sat on the ground, facing the plane, his back against the hollow tree. It would soon be dark. He lit his pipe and lifted his eyes to catch the last of the day's light draining from the sky, shot through with gold and long streaks of deep red, he thought that perhaps he had never, in all his life, seen anything quite so lovely. The children had only just left, he had to be firm with them, not wanting the darkness to fall until they were safely home. Mina's words stayed with him and he was conscious of needing – wanting – to honour them properly.

"But, but – " It was, as usual, Ruby who wanted to linger, trying to get him to tell more stories about is flying days. She had been content, for most of the day, climbing trees and acting, as Peter put it, their look-out. Mostly she had been contented with this, since she was never happier than when up above the ground, dreaming of flight, while below, the three of them measured and sawed and hammered, but, on the whole, Gabriel knew, played their game. Yet, it was – in spite of his doubts about the feasibility of it – a game of truth and honesty. Peter and Oby worked hard and well and it was satisfying to see the relationship between the two of them grow and strengthen, for he had sensed a rivalry, or at least a wariness, up until today. Something had shifted and settled and they made a good pair, with Peter all serious and steady and Oby a little wilder and with occasional unexpected flashes of humour, laughing when Peter mimicked one of their teachers.

"Maybe you could be a plane builder when you grow up, then Peter?" Oby had teased, his olive face rippled by a smile.

"A plane builder?" Peter had sat back on his heels, under one of the wings that they were starting to try and repair.

"Or a plain builder?" Oby had said, waiting for Peter to catch the joke, who when he did, flicked Oby's hair, but gently and then smiled too.

After they had all eaten the sandwiches that Ruby and Peter had brought along, and some of the blackberries, leaving their fingers stained and purple, Ruby had wandered a little way off to the edge of the clearing, promising not to climb the big pine. For a little while the three had sat talking about the next piece of repair and who would be doing what, then Ruby had suddenly re-appeared, squatting down amongst them, frowning at Gabriel and blurting out the question.

"What will you do, when you get there?"

"Home?" Saying the word aloud to these three made it both suddenly real and yet also a long way away.

Ruby nodded and Oby gave Gabriel a sharp stare as if he knew more than he could possibly know about Gabriel's past life and the past life of his country too. For a second or two, Gabriel was reminded of Mina, that same sadly accusing look.

They will never forgive, you know, they and their kind, nor forget. Herbert's voice whispered at him through the breeze-shift of leaves.

"I – " Gabriel couldn't answer.

"Go and see his mum and dad, I'd think, eh?" Peter was making a circled maze pattern in the pine needles.

"If they are still alive, I s'pose," Oby said, but not in any dark or threatening way.

"Indeed," Gabriel answered, as evenly as he could manage. Ruby hadn't finished, though.

"What about your wife?"

Peter was looking at him now, suddenly interested.

"I don't have a wife," said Gabriel.

"No wife?" Oby interrupted, and he sounded disappointed, there were few unmarried people in his community. "Maybe you'll find one," Oby added, ever practical.

"Maybe I shall," Gabriel could think of no other answer. And then the two boys had started teasing one another about the girls at school and which one they'd hate to have to marry and soon handfuls of pine needles were grabbed and there was a friendly scuffle to see who could be first to shove them down someone's neck. Then Oby chased Ruby until she shinned back up her tree again. Gabriel still sat and watched and laughed for a while, until Peter finally told everyone they should get on; for an unsettling moment Gabriel was reminded of Herbert, who had always taken the role of organiser, which was no doubt why he had ended up in command.

Herbert.

Later, when the children had gone, he would go and pay his respects and tidy the grave, marked as it was by a small cross, roughly made from two pieces of ash bound together. It could, to anyone who might see it (although this was unlikely, since the shifting dapple of the shade around it, or anyone nearby, made it hard to see) but if they did they would likely think it was the grave of a dead animal, a woodsman's dog perhaps. It was often how Gabriel tried to think of it and the thought gave him some comfort. He should tidy it, though; he didn't want Mina to bring flowers and see his neglect. On top of everything else it would make the crime – for crime it had been – seem so much harsher and she would judge him all the harder for it.

He looked up again, from his place on the floor of the wood. It really would soon be dark and he should go if he was to visit Herbert before returning to his cabin. It was later than he liked for this kind of visit because at night Herbert would often seem closer and more present, taunting him with a greater vigour. It had been Ruby who had held them all up, at first she had sat on the branch of the beech tree, pretending she couldn't hear their calls and when she had come down she had caught hold of his hand with a tender shyness that snatched at a long-ago memory of Anna.

"What is it?" He had bent down in front of her and she waited until Oby and Peter were out of earshot.

"My wings," she whispered.

He remembered, of course, he still had those swan's wings back at his cabin, she must want them returned. He had forgotten about them until now, although whenever he saw them they cheered him in his loneliness and made him believe that flight was still possible.

"You shall have them the next time you come," he smiled at her, not letting go of her hand.

"No, no." She shook her head, serious and frowning, "you don't get it. I want you to have them, you know for good luck and everything." Her big green eyes locked into his for a moment.

"Ah, I see." He understood the huge generosity this involved and was touched by it. What could he give in return? The thought ran through his mind. He had promised her flight, but – best not to go further with that one. What then? Yes, in his box, from Anna all those years ago, when he had told her what he intended and by this time she had already left him in so many different ways.

They had met outside their favourite café and had sat in the late summer light, eating apple cake and drinking coffee. It was the last time they had met in this way; they might, from the outside, be considered a couple of young lovers.

"Here." Anna had held her hand out to him, her fist closed, but gently, hiding something there. "Close your eyes and give me your hand."

A kind of hope had sprung in him then, but he knew it was false.

"There," she said, as if marking an ending, "open them

now."

He'd felt the soft flutter, like a butterfly, settle onto his palm. He opened his eyes.

"I made it," she said, smiling as one might to encourage a child.

He looked down at what he was holding: it was a butterfly, but a paper one, made from the map paper they had both used in school.

"It's beautiful," he said. And it was. So simply made, no colour, no marks at all, but in shape, form and essence a true butterfly.

"For you," she said, as she got up, ready to leave, "to keep you safe up there." She cast her eyes up at the bright sky above them. And then she left. The next and last time he'd seen her it had been by the lake. He kept the butterfly with him always, though, safe and unmarked after all these years and now he knew he must give it to Ruby. It was for the best.

"Next time you come," he said, still crouched in front of her with the boys stirring impatiently now at the clearing's edge, ready to go. "I have something to give you in return. Yes?" he smiled brightly at her to make her smile too and it worked. "To keep you safe also. Now off you go. The night will be here soon."

Making his way to Herbert's grave, Gabriel felt more lightened and unburdened than he had for a long while and for once he sang the old lullaby to himself, without fear:

> *Lee la luu*
> *Only the Man in the Moon is watching*
> *how the little babies are sleeping*
> *so, you sleep too.*

But maybe it was this that made him careless, so that he failed to notice the dark shadow dogging him as he moved through the trees.

The farm

"No, no, no!" Ruby slammed the door to her bedroom and threw herself on the bed among the hard, uncaring dolls. Mum hadn't followed, it was obvious that no one was going to say the right thing, or do the right thing and best if she was left to cry it out, it was her mum's way. And after a while, as the windows filled with dusk light and the room was masked in shadow, Ruby did get up and go and look out. First towards Peter's garden, hoping by some chance that he'd be out there, knowing she needed him, ready to swing a ladder up so she could climb down and they could both run away together, to the wood and to Gabriel. The wood: Ruby pressed her face against the glass and stared into the distance where Bower Wood was now massed like a thick and huge black fist against the palest of yellow-pink skies. Gabriel. Ruby felt tears boiling again, it wasn't fair. She clenched her hands tightly when she thought about Stan. It was him, it must have been have been him. Her mum hadn't said who, but Ruby was sure of it and Peter would be too when he found out. She must find a way of telling him, but short of jumping out of the window, there was no way she could.

Lying on her bed she held Susie Doll close and whispered to her instead; she was no substitute, but she would have to do. "Stan," she rasped into the cool china ear, "he's a tell-tale and, and – " something else, but it was hard to find the words. What had her mum said? First of all she'd been cross because Ruby and Peter were so late back, too late for Ruby to bike down to the oast with her dad's supper, like she always and forever did on a Saturday night, so Mum had to do it instead, which was a bit much after the day she'd had out in the sun picking hops and then coming home and cooking as well. Anyway, someone (Stan, it had to be) had been and told her dad about the wood and Gabriel and everything and now it was all finished. They were never allowed to go there again. Never. Her mum was going to tell Peter's mum first thing tomorrow.

"Hanging about in those woods with some tramp!"

"He's not a tramp," Ruby had shouted back, "he's not, he's not! He's Gabriel!"

"That's enough!" Her mum didn't usually get so cross and could mostly be talked round, but not this time. "Don't you understand? Haven't we always told you to be so careful?"

"But – " Ruby wanted to explain, if they knew what he was really like, how he'd been the one who'd helped her when she'd fallen from the tree, how lonely and sad he was and how they were helping him to go home, then they'd see and want to help too, she just knew it.

"No buts," Mum had said, anger creasing up her face into some stranger's face. "People like him were murdering little kiddies like you a few years ago. He shouldn't even be here!"

"It's not true! It's not true!" Ruby was shocked. What was her mum talking about? None it made any sense. And if she could just explain then everyone would see that Gabriel wanted to go home and they'd been trying to help him. But her mum's face became screwed up and tight with anger again. It was as if she'd gone mad and that was when Ruby understood it was no use and beat off up the stairs.

Curled up in her eiderdown Ruby's last thought before sleep sucked her in was that tomorrow she'd go and see Gabriel and they couldn't stop her. She'd find a way.

The camp

Mina was there early for Sunday. She often went to church in the village, but not this Sunday. There was something she must do; it had been playing on her mind. Near the camp by the river, just along from Mina's van was a small inlet and sometimes – if it had been an especially warm, dry summer, as this one had – you could walk across to a place that was normally inaccessible because of the water. It was here that a great tumble of late wild roses could be found, small faded red flowers like miniature crinolines. The thorns, though tiny, were very sharp, snagging the fingers that would try and pick them and perhaps it was this and the half-forgotten, half-hiddenness of them that meant they had survived and thrived for so long.

These were the flowers she must have, the ones she would take to Gabriel's friend's grave. And once she had decided there was little that could shift Mina. There was a sense she had that if a thing was right it must be done. The taking of the flowers must be done because she had promised and it was important, not just for this grave but for all those others too. And with the roses, once they had come into her mind, it was as if it had all been settled long ago.

What she hadn't bargained for was Ruby, crashing through the trees, wiping fresh tears from her face, breathing hard, gasping out something about Stan down on the track, scaring her, calling her dad names, dirty coward, and other words, calling Gabriel names too, full of sharpness and to do with the War. Mina calmed her, let her catch her breath again, told her not to worry, Stan was a man full of sad business.

Then Ruby saw the roses and Mina had to tell her what she was doing. The look in Ruby's eyes, the mixture of curious anxious questioning and fear; how very attached to Gabriel this child was, more than Mina had realised. They all three were, she reckoned. But wasn't this as it should be? The young making new paths for the old to follow.

"Any case, Aunty Mina," she'd said (Aunty, that warmed her), "I know exactly where it is." And that had sealed it.

"Come, then," Mina held out the roses, "you take these and I'll follow. Careful, though, the thorns are sharp."

Together they disappeared into the trees, soon becoming just another shifting ripple of shadow dipping in and out of the sun and into the dark again. Meanwhile, from down across the fields the Sunday bells rolled out their familiar call.

The hut in the wood

Gabriel stood outside his hut, lifting his face to the morning warmth, catching the far off sound of bells, reminding him that it was Sunday and filling him with a sudden longing to be inside a church again, bending down, praying – but to whom, or what? He had so long ceased to believe in such higher powers. Man it was who made the world, the goodness and the badness too, it was what war had taught him if nothing else.

He stretched his arms up and twisted his shoulders, one more winter was about all he could manage living like this. He longed too, for a soft bed and the comfort of walls. A home again with people he loved. It seemed almost feasible, infected as he was with the simple optimism that sprang so readily from Ruby, Peter and young Oby. Gabriel bent back inside to fetch his can, last time the children had brought him some coffee, or at least what passed for it, an oily liquid in a bottle with a picture of an Indian soldier on the label. It was better than nothing and what he had a taste for this morning. He'd make a fire outside too, there was just enough breeze to feed it properly and such homely tasks calmed him.

It was the crashing noise of someone running through the trees that roused him from his gentle fire tending, half mesmerized as he was from watching the flames catch and fatten into a rich and satisfying glow. Out of cautious habit, he ducked back behind the cabin, ready to run himself if need be.

"Gabriel!" A breathless shout, a familiar voice.

Gabriel came round to the front of the cabin. Peter was standing half bent and out of breath, not able to speak except for two words, "Stitch. Sorry."

Finally, after a moment, Peter straightened and stood, pale-faced and upset, close to tears, Gabriel thought, if he hadn't known him better. Peter was not a boy who would cry easily. He clasped the boy by the shoulders and patted him lightly with his fingers, trying to soothe him enough so that he could tell his story.

"Where do you think she is now?" Gabriel asked, when Peter had finished telling him how that morning Ruby had rushed round to see him and blurted out that she (and he too) were not to go to the woods again and on no account were they to visit him, Gabriel, ever, ever again either.

"I don't know," Peter shook his head, "she wasn't s'posed to be out and was going to cop it if her mum and dad knew she'd come round to my house. That's all I know. I thought she'd go back home." He shrugged and looked at Gabriel, wanting to hear from him that it was all going to be all right and that Ruby wasn't in trouble.

"And why – I wonder," Gabriel asked, but mostly to himself, he knew the answer really. He was sure he'd been followed recently and all the while he'd thought it was Herbert. What a fool he'd been! A superstitious fool. Someone, the follower someone, must have told Ruby's parents and of course they were worried. It was only natural. Why, he would have been worried too, if his child had been wandering into the forest to visit a strange man who, to the rest of the world, would appear wild and threatening, a member of the enemy tribe. Gabriel smiled a bitter smile to himself. It really was like a kind of fairytale.

"Listen," he said, "you must go home now. Yes? Perhaps Ruby is there also and all will be well."

"But – " Peter wanted to stay, he wanted Gabriel to help him search all the places in the wood where Ruby might be. She could be waiting for them now at the plane, up the tree perched in her favourite lookout spot. Surely –

"It is for the best," Gabriel was firm.

"What if," Peter tried, "what if we never see you again?"

"I am sure you will," said Gabriel, who wasn't, "but it is important that you do as your parents say."

"Yes, all right then." Peter knew when it was worth arguing.

It was obvious that Gabriel wouldn't let him stay, so maybe he was right and he should go back to the farm. Ruby was probably there; if not, and she was on her way to the wood, well, he'd meet her anyway.

"One other thing," Gabriel said. "Wait a moment, please." He went into his hut and came out holding something in his hand. "Here, Peter. I should like it very much if you would give this to Ruby. Yes?"

"If you like," Peter took the tin that had once, by the looks of it, held tobacco, but it was very old. He wondered what was inside, or if it was just the tin that Gabriel wanted him to give to Ruby. Oh, well, he thought, slipping it into his pocket, he'd find out he supposed, when he gave it to her.

"Now, you must go, I think." Gabriel was looking at him seriously and holding out his hand again, but this time for Peter to take. It seemed like a very grown-up thing shaking hands to say goodbye and when Gabriel let go he bowed his head a little to one side and seemed a "bit sad", Peter told Ruby later when he described it all to her.

"Travel safely, Peter!" Gabriel called as he waved him off down the path. "Yes?"

Peter nodded and stopped for a moment, "You too," he answered and then started running. He must find Ruby and tell her Gabriel was all right and that they would definitely see him again and she mustn't worry.

In the wood:

Mina had let Ruby run on ahead so that she could be the one who put the roses on the grave. Children, she knew, had a morbid fascination for this kind of thing and perhaps too, it was – she reasoned to herself – a way to help Ruby mark the recent and more real death of her best-loved cat. So, Mina stood well back to let Ruby feel she was the one doing the important job here. And it was touching to watch her kneeling by the grave of this man who was once an enemy and no doubt would have seen her kind as – what? She wasn't sure, but somehow she sensed that this long-dead man and Gabriel were not from the same mould. Kneeling there in the tangled shade Ruby was just a figure, a shadowed human shape, kneeling for all those unknown others in a million unmarked places. This was though, Mina thought, glancing around the fringe of trees, a lovely spot to be buried in, whatever kind of life you had led, to end it peacefully here, she'd not complain.

A noise – a cough, she couldn't be sure – made her turn her head and she saw among the many shifting, patched shadows cast by the sun's brightness, another figure and one she recognised. And the way he stood – what was he holding, pointing at the kneeling figure? "My God!" Mina's hand went to her mouth and she tried to move, but another hand pulled her back. Gabriel was suddenly there, pushing her aside, putting himself in front of Ruby, his arms stretched out wide. And when it came, the sound of the shot drummed into the still golden air of the morning, shattering the calm of this beautiful place with a deadly, almost graceful ease. Only as its echo, fattened and died away, could Mina move, running to lift a mute and rigid Ruby from where she knelt by the grave.

It was later she remembered the other man, Ruby's father, grabbing Stan by the throat and punching and punching him. But after what had happened it seemed such small thing, almost comic.

Ruby's bedroom

Down at the bottom of the garden she could just make out her dad standing, doing nothing, leaning against the stile, his back to the orchard. Behind him the geese moved together, white and ghostly, quiet for once.

Yesterday was like another place. It was mashed into a blur in Ruby's head, as if it was something she'd seen happening to someone else. How fast it had all been. One minute she was kneeling with the roses Mina had given her – the next there was shouting and screaming and Gabriel pushing her over. Next.

The bang that seemed to go on and on.

Mina, gathering her up. Angry words. Someone else falling. Her dad holding her too tight, Mina's soft voice as she knelt now beside Gabriel who lay on the ground, still as a broken branch.

How could it be? She shifted her elbows and cupped her head in her hands, pressing her nose against the cold glass. Over there, in the gathering dark was the wood, where Gabriel would stay forever and ever now. Ruby wished her dad could make a box for him too, like the one he'd made for Blackness, carving his name, plain and careful, just the same.

A great sigh heaved out of her and she saw that the glass was wet where her face had been. She closed her eyes and began to hum quietly to herself, not hearing her mum come in to see where she'd got to, scolding her gently for still being up. Drawing the curtains to shut out the night.

Paper Wings

Three weeks later and the two of them were on the Mound, sitting with their backs against the oak tree, waiting for Oby. The smell of autumn was everywhere now and even the distant glinting line of sea looked smoky and golden with the promise of the year's end.

Ruby's eyes were still red and swollen, but at least she hadn't cried today. Peter had brought one of his big handkerchiefs, though, in case, and not just for her either. He felt for it now, in his pocket, for comfort really; that's when he found it, the tin Gabriel had given him to give to Ruby. He'd forgotten all about it after what had happened. It had been Oby's Aunt Mina who'd said they shouldn't tell the police or anything like that, the gypsies weren't fond of the police poking their noses in as a general rule. Surprisingly, everyone else had gone along with it, well, everyone who knew; Ruby's mum and dad, the three of them and Stan didn't count anyway. Once he'd got up beaten and bruised, he'd cleared off sharpish; the story was he'd gone to Ireland or some place, to visit a cousin.

"Poor cousin!" Ruby said to Peter, who looked at her and smiled in that way that always forced her to smile back.

"Yeah," he said, after another quiet and comfortable moment between them, then adding that it didn't seem right that you could go round shooting people and get away with it like that. "Lucky your dad didn't kill him," he said, scrunching his own fist into a hard ball. Ruby, it could have been Ruby, buried in the cold ground now, if it hadn't been for Gabriel.

Peter fished out the tin now and gave it to Ruby who stared at it, frowning. "Gabriel gave it to me," he said, "for you." She didn't answer. Was she going to cry again? Maybe he should have waited, or given it to her mum or someone, but no, that wouldn't have been right. Gabriel had given it to him and it had been the last time he'd seen him, the last time he'd spoken to him. It seemed like years ago.

"Aren't you going to open it?" Peter was curious; having forgotten about it he now really wanted to know what it was.

Ruby opened the tin and carefully lifted out the tiny paper butterfly. "It's lovely," she whispered, holding it with same breath-held surprise he'd seen on her face when a real butterfly had settled on her hand.

Then, very gently, she threw it towards him, where it was caught and lifted in a sudden, small ripple of breeze.

"And look," she said.

Acknowledgments and big thanks to:

Andrew Barnett, Jim Benstead, Jeannie Birdsall,
Hannah Firmin, Jocelyn Goddard,
Sue Heap, Linda Newbery, Bella Pearson,
Stefan Schmidt, Ben Sharpe.

Lightning Source UK Ltd.
Milton Keynes UK
UKHW021217040321
379639UK00019B/433

9 780956 483300